# BTL MARKETING
# PLAYBOOK

## FOR YOUNG MARKETERS

### Your Essential Guide to
### On-ground Engagement
### and Measurable Impact

## RAMESH KRISH

## BTL Marketing Playbook
Copyright © 2025 Ramesh Krish

Publisher: Inkscribe Publishing Pvt. Ltd.

ISBN Number: 978-1-966421-85-6

## Disclaimer

This "BTL Marketing Playbook for Young Marketers" is intended solely as an educational resource and a practical guide for marketing professionals. The concepts, strategies, and methodologies presented herein are based on general marketing principles and the author's extensive professional experience.

All case studies, figures, statistics, budget examples, and specific data points mentioned throughout this book are provided for illustrative purposes only. These examples are fictional or simplified representations designed to demonstrate concepts and should not be interpreted as actual historical data, financial advice, or precise performance metrics from any real company or campaign. Readers should apply the principles discussed with their own discretion, conducting independent research and analysis pertinent to their specific market, industry, and business context.

The author and publisher disclaim any liability for any loss or damage, direct or indirect, arising from the use of the information contained in this playbook.

## A Note from the Author: RAMESH. K

Hello, future marketing leaders!

I'm Ramesh. K, and I have had the incredible opportunity to spend nearly 25 years navigating the exciting, challenging, and ever-evolving world of marketing across diverse sectors. My journey has taken me through the dynamic pace of Telecom and FMCG to the nuanced environments of NBFC and Retail. Along the way, I have been fortunate enough to contribute to major launches, build impactful brands, and consistently drive top-line growth.

My passion lies in Below-The-Line (BTL) marketing, because that's where the real magic happens direct connections, measurable results, and campaigns that truly resonate with people. I have spent years in the trenches, from conceptualizing and launching new products to establishing best practice standards in brand management and marketing operations. My focus has always been on crafting unique strategies that fuel marketplace presence, enhance brand visibility and loyalty, and significantly increase footfalls.

I have had the privilege of leading creative teams, managing agencies, and implementing successful ATL & BTL activities alongside social media campaigns. My expertise extends to meticulous market-wise planning and execution across both Retail and Alternate channels, ensuring every element, right down to signage, is optimized for impact.

This playbook is a distillation of that experience. It's built on the belief that effective BTL doesn't require massive budgets, but rather smart planning, creative execution, and a deep understanding of your audience. As someone who's played a key role in budgeting for annual marketing calendars, steered product enhancements, and developed comprehensive go-to-market strategies, my goal is to share these insights with you, providing practical frameworks, real-world examples, and the kind of ground-level knowledge that often isn't taught in textbooks.

I'm thrilled to guide you through the exciting world of BTL marketing and equip you with the tools to launch campaigns that don't just make noise but create lasting impact. Let's build some brilliant campaigns together!

# What You'll Discover Inside

Unlike broad, mass-reach advertising (often called Above-The-Line or ATL), BTL focuses on targeted, personal, and measurable interactions. This playbook will equip you with the essential knowledge and practical tools to master this critical domain, especially vital for industries like Telecom, NBFC, FMCG, and Retail where on-the-ground presence drives direct conversions.

Inside these chapters, you will learn:

* The "Why" and "How" of BTL: Understanding its core components and why it's a superpower for driving real business outcomes.

* Essential Tactics: A breakdown of the seven key BTL activities you will encounter and how to execute them effectively.

* Real-World Successes: Dive into practical case studies, from SIM activation blitzes to retail mall activations, giving you blueprints you can adapt.

* Ground-Level Insights: Learn the unwritten rules and practical tips that only come from hands-on experience in the field.

* Measurement & ROI: How to track your campaign's success without fancy tools and prove the tangible value of your efforts.

* The Phygital Advantage: Seamlessly blend offline hustle with online muscle by integrating digital tools into your BTL campaigns.

* Practical Planning: Step-by-step guidance on how to plan, budget, and launch your first BTL campaign, anticipating challenges before they arise.

\* Vendor Management: Your secret weapon for efficient execution, from identifying reliable partners to tracking their performance.

Your Journey to Impactful Marketing Starts Here

BTL marketing isn't just about campaigns; it's about connecting with customers on a human level. It's about being resourceful, creative, and agile. This playbook is your companion to navigating the exciting, fast-paced world of BTL, transforming you from a newcomer into an executive who consistently delivers measurable impact.

So, let's get started. Get ready to activate, engage, and convert!

# BTL Marketing Playbook for Young Marketers

## Table of Contents

*Acknowledgments*

*This book would not have been possible without the unwavering support, guidance, and inspiration of many incredible individuals.*

*First and foremost, I extend my deepest gratitude to my mentors, whose wisdom and encouragement have shaped my journey and challenged me to think beyond the ordinary. Your belief in my potential has been my driving force.*

*To my seniors, thank you for setting the benchmark of excellence and for your constant guidance that helped me navigate through complexities with confidence.*

*To my wonderful colleagues, your collaboration, camaraderie, and constructive feedback added immense value to this work. Working alongside you has been both enriching and fulfilling.*

*To my family — your unconditional love, patience, and support have been my anchor. Thank you for standing by me through every late night and every early morning. Your faith kept me going.*

*This book is as much yours as it is mine.*

*With heartfelt gratitude,*

*Ramesh Krish*

# Chapter 1: Hey There, Marketer! (Introduction)

## 👋 Welcome to the World of BTL Marketing

So, you've just stepped into the marketing world, and someone tossed around the term BTL. Maybe you nodded like you knew what they meant (we've all done it!). But now you're curious:

What exactly is BTL marketing, and why does everyone talk about it like it's the secret sauce to getting things done?

Let's break it down — no jargon, just plain speak.

## 🎯 What Is BTL?

BTL stands for Below The Line marketing. Unlike TV ads, newspaper spreads, or YouTube prepolls (that's ATL or Above The Line), BTL is the stuff that happens on the ground, face-to-face, and direct.

Think of BTL like this:

The person giving out free shampoo samples at your local supermarket? BTL.

The gold loan company setting up a tent at your village festival? BTL.

The telecom brand doing an activation at a college fest? Yep. BTL.

BTL = targeted + personal + measurable.

💬 Quick Comparison: ATL vs. BTL vs. TTL

| Type | Stands For | Example | Used When You Want To... |
|------|-----------|---------|--------------------------|
| ATL | Above the Line | TV, Radio, Newspaper | Create mass awareness |
| BTL | Below the Line | Activations, Sampling, Direct Mail | Drive engagement & conversions |
| TTL | Through the Line | Mix of both, like QR code on a TV ad | Blend awareness + action |

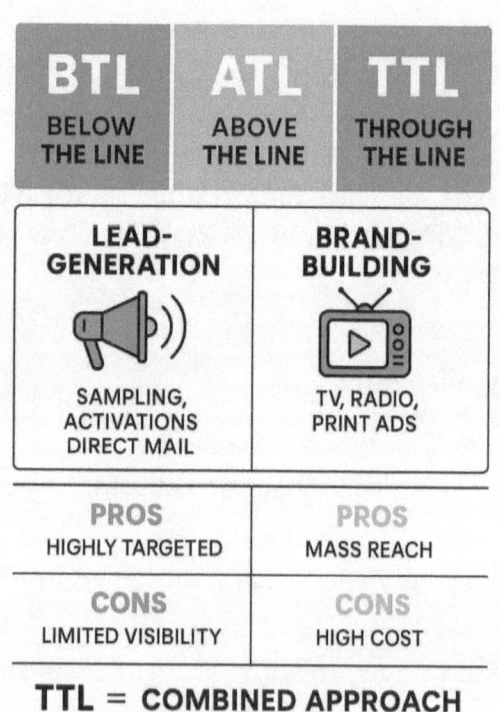

## ※ Why BTL is a Superpower (Especially for New Execs)

BTL is where the action is – where brands connect with real people and drive real results. For industries like:

Telecom: where physical presence is key to drive new SIM activations or device plans.

NBFC: where trust is built one customer at a time, especially for gold loans, microfinance, etc.

FMCG: where product trial and impulse purchases are everything.

Retail: where store footfall and last mile conversion win the game.

BTL lets you see your impact almost immediately – no more waiting 3 months to know if your ad worked.

Quick Wins of BTL:

Lower cost, higher focus

Hyper targeted (location, income group, age)

Easy to measure ROI

Builds community level engagement

Real Talk

If ATL is like shouting into a stadium, BTL is like whispering into someone's ear – it's intimate, it's local, it sticks.

So, whether you're planning a chai tapri engagement or a college roadshow, BTL is your canvas.

## ☑ What You'll Learn in This Book

What types of BTL campaigns exist and how to run them

How to plan smartly, even with limited budgets

Real-life success stories from industries you're stepping into

Templates, checklists, and hacks that'll make you look like a pro

# Chapter 2: BTL 101 – What Counts as BTL Marketing?

Let's break it down, minus the marketing jargon.

So You're Told to "Do Some BTL" – But What Does That Mean?

Picture this:

Your brand launches a new mobile data pack, a gold loan scheme, a chocolate bar, or a summer sale. You're not going to put it on TV (too expensive), or on a hoarding (too broad). Instead, you head where the actual customers are—college campuses, market streets, Kirana stores, mobile recharge shops.

This is BTL in action. It's focused, ground level marketing where the message travels directly from your brand to the consumer—with no middleman media.

Types of BTL Activities You Should Know

Here are the most common and powerful BTL formats, explained with simple examples and industry relevance:

## 1. On Ground Activations

These are the bread and butter of BTL.

What It Is: Small branded stalls, kiosks, or setups in high footfall areas where you interact with consumers directly.

FMCG: Sampling flavoured milk at school gates.

NBFC: Setting up a gold loan counter at a rural market.

Retail: Try & Buy stalls outside a mall.

Telecom: SIM activations at bus stands or haats.

Pro Tip: Always have a loud yet friendly promoter and a call to action (form fill, freebie, QR scan).

## 2. In Store Branding

If your product is sold in shops, this one is gold.

• What It Is: Using point of sale (POS) materials like danglers, posters, shelf strips, standees, and display racks to grab attention.

FMCG: Branded racks in a Kirana store with your biscuits or juices.

Telecom: Recharge desk branding with new data plan stickers.

Retail: Mirrors that say, "New Collection Just Landed!"

NBFC: Desk branding in partner jewellery stores for gold loans.

Pro Tip: Keep it simple, local language friendly, and visible at the eye level.

## 3. Direct Marketing

This is where you go to the customer with the message.

• What It Is: Door to door leaflets, WhatsApp broadcasts, emailers, or cold calling with targeted offers.

NBFC: Sending gold rate alerts via SMS/WhatsApp.

FMCG: Coupons distributed in apartment societies.

Telecom: Re targeting inactive customers with win back offers.

Retail: VIP invitations to top shoppers for preview sales.

Pro Tip: Personalization wins. "Hi Priya, this plan's just for you" > "Dear Customer…"

## 4. Sampling Campaigns

Let them taste, smell, feel or use your product.

⦿ What It Is: Giving away product samples at events, stores, schools, traffic signals, etc.

🥤 FMCG: Tasting counters at college fests.

👕 Retail: Free perfume trials in a fashion store.

🧴 NBFC: Loan preapproval slips at temples (yes, it works!)

▦ Telecom: SIM + ₹20 talk time giveaways at rural events.

💡 Pro Tip: Get feedback immediately— "How was the taste?" "Would you buy this?"

## 5. Roadshows & Mobile Vans

Take your brand on the move.

⦿ What It Is: A branded vehicle with music, branding, a mic, and promoters—moving across towns or neighbourhoods.

🥤 FMCG: Ice cream truck style tasting drives.

▦ Telecom: 4G awareness vans in tier 3 towns.

🧴 NBFC: Loan awareness drives with street plays.

👕 Retail: Announcing discounts and store openings.

💡 Pro Tip: Combine roadshows with leafleting and games for better footfall.

## 6. Event Sponsorships & College Activations

Where there's a crowd, there's your chance.

● What It Is: Tying up with a local event to display your brand, put up a stall, or run a contest.

▦ Telecom: Free charging stations at college fests.

▪ FMCG: Sponsoring a football match with free drinks.

▪ NBFC: Career fair stalls promoting educational loans.

☎ Retail: Spot styling contests or brand ambassadors.

♀ Pro Tip: Choose events where your target audience naturally gathers. Don't just go for "bigger crowd = better."

## 7. Influencer & Hyperlocal Engagement

Not all influencers have blue ticks!

● What It Is: Tie ups with local leaders, society heads, store managers, or micro influencers to spread your brand message.

▪ NBFC: Local jewellery shop endorsing your gold loan scheme.

▪ FMCG: Home chef promoting your cooking oil in a community WhatsApp group.

☎ Retail: Tailors or stylists recommending your store.

▦ Telecom: Local "tech geek" recommending your recharge plans.

♀ Pro Tip: Local trust beats national celebrity endorsement when it comes to BTL.

💬 Quick Recap Table

| Activity Type | Where It Happens | Best For |
|---|---|---|
| Activations | Marketplaces, Malls | All industries |
| In store Branding | Shops, Retail Chains | FMCG, Retail |
| Direct Marketing | Homes, Phones | NBFC, Telecom |
| Sampling | Events, Stores | FMCG |
| Roadshows | Rural/Urban Areas | Telecom, FMCG |
| Sponsorships | Colleges, Events | All industries |
| Local Engagement | Communities | NBFC, Retail |

🎯 Takeaway for Newbies:

> Don't just ask "What BTL should I do?"

> Ask "Where is my customer hanging out today, and how can I connect with them without shouting?"

# Chapter 3: Planning Like a Pro (Even If You're New)

How to go from "I think we need a promo" to "We nailed that campaign!"

### The Truth About Planning in BTL

In BTL, you don't just "think" and "create" like an ATL agency. You plan, juggle, adapt, and sometimes even carry standees in the rain. But trust us—it's fun, fast paced, and incredibly satisfying.

A well planned BTL campaign feels like pulling off a live performance—with the crowd clapping at the end (and filling your lead sheet).

Here's how to plan one like a pro:

### Step 1: Know Exactly What You're Solving For

Before jumping into tents, banners, and budgets, ask:

What's the goal?

Awareness? (E.g., a new branch opening?)

Lead generation? (E.g., for a loan product or telecom plan?)

Sales push? (E.g., FMCG sampling or retail clearance?)

Loyalty or recall? (E.g., styling booths or games?)

Pro Tip: Write your goal on a sticky note and check every plan against it. If it doesn't serve the goal, toss it

## 👤 Step 2: Get into Your Customer's Shoes

Don't just guess— observe.

Where do they shop, travel, wait, hang out?

What do they like—freebies, games, info, discounts?

Do they prefer WhatsApp or printed flyers? QR or SMS?

🛍 FMCG: If your TG is students → college fests, coaching centres.

💰 NBFC: Housewives → temples, ration shops, society noticeboards.

📶 Telecom: Youth and migrant workers → recharge shops, bus stands.

👕 Retail: Working professionals → metros, office hubs, gyms.

🔒 Pro Tip: Go visit the place before finalizing your activity. You'll discover more in 10 minutes there than 3 hours on PowerPoint.

## 💰 Step 3: Budget Like You're Paying from Your Pocket

It's easy to get carried away with flashy setups. But BTL is about impact per money spent.

Create a basic budget like this:

| Item | Approx Cost (per day) | Notes |
|---|---|---|
| Promoter (1 person) | ₹800–₹1,200 | Language fluency matters |
| Canopy / Table Setup | ₹1,500–₹2,500 | Includes basic branding |
| Leaflets (1,000 pcs) | ₹700–₹900 | Local language preferred |
| QR Code Printing | ₹ 200 | Trackable & cheap |
| Sampling Material | Varies | Product dependent |
| Permissions (if needed) | ₹500–₹1,000 | Municipality, RWAs etc. |
| Data Entry + CRM follow up | ₹500–₹800 | Optional but useful |

🔒 Pro Tip: Always keep 10–15% aside as "buffer". BTL is unpredictable—extra print, sudden rains, etc.

## Step 4: Create a Killer Campaign Brief (Your Bible)

This is where many first timers mess up: No brief = confused vendors = messy execution.

Your brief should answer:

1. What are we promoting?

2. Who are we targeting?

3. Where will the activity happen?

4. When will it start and end?

5. What will the promoter say/do/give?

6. What does success look like? (e.g., 500 leads, 100 conversions)

7. Contact person & escalation matrix

**Pro Tip:** Add reference photos or sketches. Visuals avoid a ton of miscommunication.

## Step 5: Choose the Right Location (With Logic)

Your budget is limited, so go where:

There's high relevant footfall

The audience is idle (e.g., waiting in lines, resting in parks, commuting)

You can legally & practically set up

Don't just go where the crowd is. Go where the right crowd is.

FMCG: School gate at 3 PM > Highway billboard

NBFC: Monthly ration shop day > Fancy mall

Telecom: Long distance bus stop > College tech event

Retail: Gym reception > Bus shelter

**Pro Tip:** Run a pilot in one area first before rolling out to 20 cities.

## Step 6: Set SMART Metrics

Your boss will ask: What did we get out of this?

So, you must define:

   Reach (how many people saw/interacted)

   Leads (how many showed interest/shared contact)

   Conversions (how many took action—bought, activated)

   Cost per lead/conversion (efficiency)

Pro Tip: Use QR codes, manual registers, Google Forms, and CRM tools to track data in real time.

## Final Checklist Before Kick Off

[1] Campaign brief shared with all vendors & teams

[2] Permissions taken for location (police, local body, society etc.)

[3] Branding collaterals printed and tested

[4] Promoter training done (scripts + FAQs)

[5] Sampling stock packed and labelled

[ 6] Live tracking link (if using) tested

[ 7] Contingency kit packed (rain cover, first aid, extra flyers)

## Your First Campaign Will Teach You More Than Any Book

It won't be perfect. There will be something forgotten, a vendor delay, or feedback that stings. And that's exactly how you grow.

# Chapter 4: Tools of the Trade – Your BTL Toolkit

Because duct tape and Excel sheets alone won't get you very far.

## 💼 You Don't Need Fancy Gadgets—Just Smart Ones

BTL marketing is boots on ground stuff. You don't always have swanky ad agencies and big studios. What you do have is hustle—and the right tools to manage chaos efficiently.

Here's your toolkit for executing killer BTL campaigns—whether you're promoting telecom in Tamil Nadu, selling soap in Surat, or pushing loans in Lucknow.

## 🔧 1. Promoter Kit (The Field Force Arsenal)

Your promoter is your brand face. Equip them well:

| Tool | Why It Matters |
|---|---|
| Branded T shirt / Cap | Consistent identity, visibility |
| Canopy / Umbrella Setup | Mobile, easy branding + shade |
| Flyers / Leaflets | Basic info, offer details, QR codes |
| Sampling Tray / Kit | Product trials (for FMCG especially) |
| Pitch Card / FAQs Sheet | Answers common questions confidently |
| Data Collection Sheet /App | To gather leads (manual/Google Form/CRM |
| WhatsApp/Call Scripts | Ready to use talk tracks for lead follow |
| Feedback Slips (Optional) | Capture reactions and objections |

🔒 Pro Tip: Always have a spare kit in your local office or branch in case of emergency.

## ▥ 2. Tech Tools That'll Save Your Life

BTL campaigns can get messy without tracking. These apps help you stay in control:

| Tool/App | Use Case |
| --- | --- |
| Google Forms | Lead capture, promoter check ins, quick surveys |
| Canva | Instant poster, banner, and flyer design |
| Trello / Notion | Campaign planning, task tracking |
| WhatsApp Business | Customer response, bulk messaging with tags |
| SurveyMonkey / Type form | Customer feedback & reporting |
| Zoho CRM / Lead squared | Lead nurturing and follow up workflows |
| Tally Counter App | Counting footfalls and samples given |
| Drive / Dropbox | Share artwork, briefing kits with vendors easily |

🔒 Pro Tip: Set up a shared drive folder for each campaign with subfolders: "Creative", "Promoters", "Daily Reports", "Permissions".

## 🎨 3. Creative Collaterals That Work (and What Doesn't)

Your customer gives you 3 seconds. Use them well.

| Collateral | Must Haves |
| --- | --- |
| Flyers | Local language, offer clearly visible, QR code |
| Standees | Should say what, why, and how in 7 words max |
| Posters | Use at eye level, simple message, bold visuals |
| Banners | For canopies, shops, counters – readable from 10 ft |
| Shelf Strips | For FMCG visibility inside Kirana/general stores |
| Stickers | Mobile recharges, shop windows, loan counters |
| Giveaway Cards | Coupons, "Refer a Friend", "Call for Offer" cards |

✖ Avoid: Overcrowded text, dark fonts on dark backgrounds, jargon like "innovative 360 activation" (just say "Free Sample!" instead 😊 )

## 4.  Vendor Roster: Who Does What

You'll often need local vendors who can act fast and understand regional dynamics.

| Vendor Type | What They Handle |
|---|---|
| Fabricator / Printer | Canopies, danglers, standees, flex boards |
| Promoter Agency | Field staff hiring, training, and payments |
| Sampling Distributor | Inventory stocking, wastage tracking |
| Event Agency | Setup, stage, sound, permissions (for bigger gigs) |
| Data Entry / CRM Ops | Cleaning up leads, making it CRM ready |

**Pro Tip:**  Always have 2 vendors on standby. Also, do a dry run or mock setup before day one.

## 5.  Time Saving Templates (Copy Paste Ready)

Here are a few cheat code templates every BTL executive should have:

- Promoter Brief Template
- Daily Activity Tracker (Excel / Google Sheet)
- FAQ Sheet for Field Use
- Campaign ROI Calculator
- End of Campaign Summary PPT Template

🔃 Optional but Amazing Add Ons

If your brand can afford it, consider:

- 📷 Promoter Selfies for Attendance Tracking
- 💬 QR based Product Info (videos linked)
- 🎮 Interactive Games (Spin the Wheel, Lucky Dip)
- 💬 Chatbots for Instant Customer Support

💬 Takeaway for Newbies:

> "The more you prepare offline, the better you perform online (and on ground)."

You don't need a million tools—just the right ones. Focus on clarity, consistency, and speed.

# Chapter 5: Execution on the Ground – The Real Game Begins

When the sun's up, your promoter's late, and the police ask for a letter—you stay cool and crush it.

## The Day Has Come – Now What?

You've planned everything—briefing done, collaterals printed, budget approved. But trust us: BTL doesn't follow a script. Your superpower is adaptability.

This chapter helps you handle:

- People

- Promoters

- Last minute curveballs

- On ground data

- Stakeholder expectations

### Step 1: Show Up First, Always

Be the first one on site. You'll:

✅ See if setup is on time

✅ Spot issues before they explode

✅ Be the brand's eyes and ears

### Pro Tip: Carry a campaign "Go Bag":

Power bank, masking tape, scissors, pens, a few extra flyers, promoter ID tags, and a mini umbrella.

## 👥 Step 2: Managing Promoters Like A Pro

Promoters are the face of your campaign. But they're human—new, nervous, maybe even sleepy 😴.

Here's your checklist:

☑ Promoter Checklist:

- In uniform and cleanly dressed
- Knows the brand name and product benefit
- Smiling and making eye contact
- Can explain the offer clearly in local language
- Knows who to escalate issues to

🎤 Sample Pitch for Telecom:

> "Hello! We're from XYZ. This new SIM gives you 1.5 GB/day for just ₹199. You also get free caller tunes. Want to activate one today?"

🔒 Pro Tip:  Role play pitches with them before the crowd arrives. Give live feedback.

## ⚪ Step 3: Set Up Like a Brand, not a Bazaar

Your stall/kiosk/activation must look:

Clean and clutter free

Easy to approach

Branded at 3 levels: top (banner), eye level (standee), and tabletop (flyers)

⊙ Aim for a "pause point" setup—where people stop walking to look.

📱 FMCG Example:  Cold drink sampling under a blue umbrella + "Taste It Free" poster

🪙 NBFC Example:  Loan consultation table near a jewellery store with "Gold Ka Sahi Daam" dangler

📱 Retail Example:  Try on mirror corner with "Style Yourself Here" board

▦ Telecom Example:  Promoter with a recharge booklet and SIM card pouch hanging visibly

📊 Step 4: Track Everything (Or It Didn't Happen)

If you're not measuring it, you're not managing it.

Use a simple  Daily Activity Tracker:

| Time | Footfall | Interactions | Leads Captured | Sales/ Conversions | Remarks |
|---|---|---|---|---|---|
| 10am– 12pm | 45 | 22 | 8 | 1 | Peak crowd at 11am |

🔧 Tools you can use:

Google Form on phone (connected to Drive)

Tally counters

WhatsApp photo updates (timestamped)

End of day selfie reports with location tag

🔒 Pro Tip:  Ask promoters to note why people said NO. These insights are gold.

## ⚠ Step 5: Handle On Ground Issues Calmly

You will face hiccups. Here's a survival guide:

| Problem | Fix |
|---|---|
| Promoter no show | Keep a backup from your agency OR call a local temp urgently |
| Rain / Wind | Move under shade, plastic wrap materials, hand out umbrellas |
| Police or society asking for permission | Always carry a permission printout + soft copy |
| Stock delay | Redirect to nearby backup stall OR switch to lead collection |
| Customer resistant | Don't push—smile, thank, move on. BTL is not door to door sales |

🔒 Pro Tip: Always call your reporting manager once a day with status—even if all is well. It builds trust.Take the trust of Local Sales team as well.Create a rapport with them to avoid unnecessary escalations.

## 📄 Step 6: Daily Reporting That Makes You Look Like a Rockstar

Send a simple  Evening Update  to your boss:

📍 Location: MG Road Metro Exit 1

👥 Footfall: 300

💬 Interactions: 142

📞 Leads Captured: 48

🔋 Conversions (SIM Activated): 12

🕶 Insights: Best crowd between 5–7PM. Many students asked about 5G plans. Rain delay between 2–3PM.

📷 Photos Attached: Yes

🔒 Pro Tip:  Use visuals. Send 2–3 good photos from different angles. Bosses love proof.

## Real Life Mini Case Studies (From the Field)

### FMCG Sampling – "Juice for the Win!"

Brand:   Local mango drink

Location:   Tier 2 schools in Andhra Pradesh

Execution:   Sampling during lunch hours + contest "Draw Your Favourite Mango Moment"

Result:   22% sales increase in nearby Kirana stores within 2 weeks

Success Tip:  Involve school teachers—they act as BTL influencers.

### Telecom Lead Drive – "SIM, Smile, Repeat"

Brand:   Regional telecom player

Location:   Rural market in Bihar

Execution:   Branded van + promoters distributing SIMs with 2GB free data

Result:   2,000 activations in 5 days

Success Tip:  Local language pitch + free earphones as a hook.

### NBFC Gold Loan Push – "Temple Activation"

Brand:   NBFC in Kerala

Location:   Outside 4 temples during festival season

Execution:   Free water bottles + gold loan leaflets + QR scan booth

Result:   ₹2.5 Cr disbursed in loans in 3 weeks

Success Tip:  Combine utility (water) with value info (loan rates).

### Big Takeaway:

> You don't need to be perfect. You just need to be present, responsive, and hungry to learn.

# Chapter 6: BTL Case Studies & Campaign Blueprints

Copy them. Remix them. Outdo them.

## Format We'll Use for Each Case Study:

| 🔍 | Details |
|---|---|
| ⊙ Objective | What is the campaign |
| 👥 Target Group | Who they targeted |
| 📍 Location | Where it happened |
| ⚙ Activities | What BTL methods |
| ⸱ Budget | Approximate cost |
| 🗒 Outcome | Tangible results |
| 💡 Key Learnings | Tips you can use |

## Case Study 1: Telecom – SIM Card Activations in Small Towns

| 🔍 | Details |
|---|---|
| ⊙ Objective | Boost new SIM activations in Tier 3 towns |
| 👥 Target Group | Daily wage workers, youth, migrant labour |
| 📍 Location | Railway stations, bus stands in Bihar and UP |
| ⚙ Activities | Canopy setups + recharge agents + "Free 1GB + Free Earphones " offer + demo of sim features) |
| ⸱ Budget | ₹2.2 lakhs for 5 towns over 7 days |
| 🗒 Outcome | 7,300 leads collected: 2,800 activations (38% Conversions) |
| 💡 Key Learnings | Train promoters to speak the local dialect. Freebies with Immediate value (like earphones) |

## Case Study 2: NBFC – Gold Loan Festive Campaign

| 🔍 | Details |
|---|---|
| 🎯 Objective | Increase footfall and disbursement at rural branches |
| 👥 Target Group | Women & elderly in farming communities |
| 📍 Location | Village temples and weekly markets in Kerala |
| ⚙️ Activities | Mobile loan desk + free health checkup camp + leaflet distribution + water bottle branding |
| ⟋ Budget | ₹4 lakhs for 20 locations |
| 🗒 Outcome | ₹5.6 Cr gold loan disbursed in 3 weeks; 1,200 new leads |
| 💡 Key Learnings | Combine social service (like free health camp) with brand intent The trust factor in rural markets |

## Case Study 3: FMCG – Sampling in College Fests

| 🔍 | Details |
|---|---|
| 🎯 Objective | Create buzz and trials for a new flavoured milk product |
| 👥 Target Group | Students aged 15–22 |
| 📍 Location | College fests in Coimbatore and Madurai |
| ⚙️ Activities | Sampling booth + selfie zone with the brand mascot + lucky draw contest on insta |
| ⟋ Budget | ₹1.2 lakhs for 4 fests |
| 🗒 Outcome | 18,000 samples distributed; 4,300 tagged Insta posts; 11% hike in nearby store sales |
| 💡 Key Learnings | Youth = photo first, product second. Link offline BTL to online buzz. Keep branding quirky |

## Case Study 4: Retail – Store Footfall Drive

| 🔍 | Details |
|---|---|
| 🎯 Objective | Increase weekend footfall in retail apparel outlets |
| 👥 Target Group | Urban working women (25–40) |
| 📍 Location | Metro exits, office complexes, kids' play zones |
| ⚙️ Activities | Coupon distribution + "Try & Win" mirror booth outside malls + WhatsApp QR scanner for offer |
| ✎ Budget | ₹90,000 per city (including promoter + print + digital link setup) |
| 🗒 Outcome | 1,500 store visits; ₹6.2 lakhs in weekend billing; 21% redemption of coupons |
| 💡 Key Learnings | Blend physical BTL with mobile convenience. Use QR led coupons - easier to track and redeem |

## Bonus Blueprint: Zero Budget BTL Idea

| 🔍 | Details |
|---|---|
| 🎯 Objective | Create brand visibility for a new detergent |
| 👥 Target Group | Housewives in urban low-income homes |
| 📍 Location | Community washing areas in Mumbai chawls |
| ⚙️ Activities | Painted walls with soap demo + branded buckets as giveaways + promoter showing cleaning test |
| ✎ Budget | ₹25,000 total |
| 🗒 Outcome | 10,000+ impressions; 500+ inquiries to local retailer; ₹1.5L initial sales |
| 💡 Key Learnings | Local relevance wins. No stage, no banners—just product + smart context = impact |

## Summary Table – Snapshot of Campaigns

| Sector | Objective | Key Activity | Cost (₹) | Result Highlight |
|--------|-----------|--------------|----------|------------------|
| Telecom | SIM Activation | Canopy + Freebie + Pitch | 2.2L | 2,800 activations |
| NBFC | Loan Disbursal | Mobile booth + Water Kit | 4L | ₹5.6 Cr loans |
| FMCG | Product Trials | Sampling + Insta Contest | 1.2L | 11% sales spike |
| Retail | Store Footfall | QR coupon + Mirror Booth | 90K | ₹6.2L weekend sales |

## Steal This Structure Blueprint Template

Want to design your own campaign? Just follow this:

1. Objective: What are we solving?
2. Audience: Who do we want to reach?
3. Where: What's the best real-world touchpoint?
4. What: What will people see/receive/engage with?
5. Budget: What's realistic?
6. Tracking: How will we know it worked?
7. Learnings: What to note for future?

Pro Tip: Use this for every new campaign pitch—it works across all industries.

# Chapter 7: Measuring Impact – Proving That BTL Works

Because if it can't be measured, it never happened.

## 🎯 Why This Chapter Matters

As a new executive, your ideas may be awesome—but leadership trusts numbers.

BTL doesn't always have a direct sales number like digital ads, but we can still measure success using clear, creative KPIs.

Let's break it down.

### ✎ 1. Set Goals Before Execution

BTL can aim to:

Generate   leads

Drive   sales

Increase   footfall

Create   awareness

Improve   sampling

Trigger   app installs

Drive   walks ins or redemptions

👉 So, start with a number:

"We aim to collect 2,000 leads in 5 days."

"We target ₹10L gold loan disbursal from this campaign."

"We want 1,500 customers to redeem QR coupons this weekend."

## 2. Common BTL KPIs to Track

Here's a handy list of what you can and should measure:

| Metric | What It Tells You | Ideal Tools |
|---|---|---|
| Footfall | How many people passed by | Tally counter, Google Form |
| Interactions | How many people engaged with the brand | Promoter logs |
| Leads Generated | How many gave you contact/info | Forms, QR codes |
| Conversion Rate | % of leads that converted | Lead tracker + CRM |
| Sampling Distributed | How many samples were given | Count based log |
| Redemptions | How many offers/coupons used | Store POS or QR scans |
| Cost per Lead/Activation | Efficiency of spend | Budget sheet vs results |
| Social Media Engagement | Posts tagged, shares, likes | Hashtag tracking |
| Brand Recall | Pre/post surveys | Google Forms, short polls |

## 3. Examples from Real Campaigns

| Campaign | KPI Measured | Result |
|---|---|---|
| Telecom SIM Drive | Conversions | 2,800 activations from 7,300 leads - 38 % |
| FMCG Sampling + Insta Game | Insta mentions | 4,300 tagged posts in 4 college fests |
| NBFC Gold Loan Activation | Disbursal Volume | ₹5.6 Cr disbursed from 1,200 leads |
| Retail Coupon QR Redemption | Footfall uplift | 21% coupon redemption over 3 days |

## 📈 4. Dashboards That Impress Bosses

Don't wait for your manager to ask. Send a  one pager dashboard  at campaign end:

Simple BTL Campaign Report Snapshot

...

📍 Location: Cochin Lulu Mall

📅 Dates: 2–5 May 2025

👥 Footfall: 5,200

💬 Interactions: 3,600

📞 Leads: 1,020

☑ Conversions: 340 SIM activations

📊 Conversion Rate: 33.3%

💸 Spend: ₹1.8 Lakhs

🎯 Cost/Activation: ₹529

📷 Attachments: 3 images, promoter video

💡 Insight: Women aged 25–35 was most responsive. Evening slots (5–7PM) performed best.

...

🔒 Pro Tip:  Use icons, bold stats, and bullets. Don't over write.

## 5. Basic ROI Formula (No MBA Needed)

Return on Investment (ROI) =

(Value of Output – Cost of Campaign) / Cost of Campaign

Example:

Campaign cost = ₹2,00,000

Revenue from activations = ₹6,00,000

ROI = (6L – 2L) / 2L = 2 or 200%

Even in lead gen models:

> Value of Output  can be:

> Estimated lifetime value per customer × Number of conversions

🔒 **Pro Tip:** If you don't have revenue numbers, show  Cost per Lead or  Cost per Conversion.

## 6. Intangible Wins – Don't Miss These!

Not all wins are numeric. Add a slide on:

- ☑ Improved brand recall ("People already knew our name")
- ☑ Better promoter performance (after training)
- ☑ Positive customer feedback
- ☑ Increased local partnerships (e.g. stores wanting to tie up)
- ☑ PR or social media buzz

🔒 **Pro Tip:** Attach  video testimonials  or  WhatsApp chat screenshots  from real users.

## 7. Feedback Loop – Don't Just Report, Improve

Ask yourself:

What worked? (Keep doing it)

What flopped? (Fix it or dump it)

What surprised you? (That's your next insight)

Use a table like:

| What Worked | What Didn't | Next Time We'll... |
|---|---|---|
| QR code couponing | Morning footfall low | Focus on evening shift |
| Regional language | Too much print | Use voice notes |

### Real Talk from a First Time Executive

> "My first BTL campaign had 3 leads and 400 flyers in the gutter. I cried.

> My second campaign had 150 leads and 23 sales. I smiled. I learned."

> — Divya, Field Exec, FMCG Brand

BTL is trial and error. Reporting is how you   learn faster than your competitors.

# Chapter 8: Budgeting for BTL – Where Every Rupee Counts

Low budget? No problem. Low planning? Big problem.

## Why Budgeting Is Crucial in BTL

Unlike digital, BTL doesn't come with auto billing or dashboards. Every single rupee you spend is physical—print, promoter, stall, logistics. You mess up the budget, you mess up the campaign.

Let's walk through how to:

Break down BTL costs

Build a zero-waste budget

Track spending smartly

Use hacks to save more

## 1. Standard BTL Cost Heads

Here's what typically eats up your budget:

| Cost Head | Description | Sample Cost (₹) |
|---|---|---|
| Promoters | People who engage with public | ₹800–₹1,200/day/pax |
| Standees/Banners | Physical branding material | ₹150–₹500 each |
| Printing (leaflets) | Flyers, brochures | ₹1.5–₹2.5 per piece |
| Canopy/Setup Rental | Stall/kiosk setup for outdoor campaigns | ₹2,000–₹5,000/day |
| Travel & Logistics | Local transport, fuel, parking | ₹1,000–₹2,000/day |
| Freebies/Giveaways | Earphones, samples, coupons | ₹10–₹50 per unit |
| Permissions | Police/NOC/local authority | ₹500–₹5,000 per area |
| Agency Fee (optional) | If outsourced | 10–15% of total cost |
| Tech Tools | QR setup, forms, mobile recharge, etc. | ₹300–₹1,001 |

Pro Tip: Always keep a 10–15% contingency buffer.

## 2. Sample Budget – Gold Loan BTL Drive (2 Days, 1 Branch)

| Item | Units | Unit Cost (₹) | Total (₹) |
|---|---|---|---|
| Promoters (2) | 2 days | ₹ 1,000 | ₹ 4,000 |
| Leaflets | 1,000 pcs | ₹ 2 | ₹ 2,000 |
| Canopy rental | 1 | ₹ 3,000 | ₹ 3,000 |
| Branding & banners | 3 units | ₹ 300 | ₹ 900 |
| Travel & food | Lumpsum | | ₹ 1,500 |
| Freebie (Water Bottles) | 300 pcs | ₹ 8 | ₹ 2,400 |
| QR setup & forms | | | ₹ 1,000 |
| Contingency (10%) | | | ₹ 1,480 |
| Total | | | ₹ 16,280 |

If you generated even  40 leads  from this activity, that's ₹407 per lead—a decent CPL for NBFC.

### 3. Budget Planning Checklist (Quick & Dirty)

☑ Have you listed all materials and people involved?

☑ Have you taken at least 2–3 vendor quotes?

☑ Are travel/logistics accounted for?

☑ Do you have room for emergency spends (rain, police, etc.)?

☑ Have you pre-approved the spend internally?

🔒 Pro Tip:  For larger brands, get a pre signed "umbrella budget" (say ₹50,000/month for routine BTL)—it saves time on small approvals.

## 4. Budget Saving Hacks

| Problem | Hack |
|---|---|
| High printing cost | Use black & white flyers or double sided A4s |
| Expensive promoters | Hire college interns (with training) |
| Travel eats up money | Group locations by route or use e bikes |
| Wasted giveaways | Replace with on spot scratch cards or QR coupons |
| Costly permissions | Use semiprivate venues (cafes, store fronts) |
| Freelancers costing more | Outsource only creative work, not field ops |

## 5. Tools You Can Use

Google Sheets  – For budget tracker templates

Split wise/Zoho Expense  – To record team spends daily

Formstack or JotForm  – For tracking expenses tied to outcomes

WhatsApp group  – Quick expense receipts from field team

Pro Tip:  Ask field team to WhatsApp daily spend photos with captions (fuel bills, banner pics)—use it for your final report.

## 6. Budget vs ROI Dashboard Example

| Metric | Value |
|---|---|
| Total Budget | ₹ 18,000 |
| Leads Collected | 120 |
| Walk ins to Branch | 55 |
| Disbursal (₹) | ₹8.3 Lakhs |
| Cost per Lead | ₹ 150 |
| ROI | 361% |

Bonus Insight:  Walk ins mostly between 11:30–1 PM and again 4:30–6 PM. Target these slots next time.

✓ Final Tips for New Execs

1. Negotiate everything —from banner print to stall rent.

2. Pre book vendors in advance   to save costs.

3. Track daily spends —don't wait till the end.

4. Align budget to outcome —don't overspend on low impact things like balloon arches.

5. Keep proof of spend —especially for audits or director reviews.

## Chapter 9: Field Execution – The BTL Playbook for the Streets

If you can survive field execution, you're a real marketer.

### Why This Chapter Matters

All the strategy, creative, budgeting—it's nothing if  your promoter can't explain your product  or your canopy collapses in the wind.

This chapter is your cheat sheet for  flawless BTL execution

### 1. Before You Hit the Ground

Pre Execution Checklist (One Week Prior):

- ☑ Finalize location + take permission if required
- ☑ Book promoters + confirm reporting time
- ☑ Print materials (with 2-day buffer)
- ☑ Confirm delivery of branding (banners, standees)
- ☑ Prepare daily activity tracker
- ☑ Assign SPOC (you or someone you trust)
- ☑ Inform local branch/store (if joint activity)
- ☑ WhatsApp group created with all field members

Pro Tip:  Pack an emergency kit—cello tape, zip ties, scissors, extra pens, and snacks.

## 👥 2. Promoter Management 101

Your promoter is your brand's face for that customer. One bad promoter = 50 missed leads.

What You Must Do:

Brief them thoroughly (don't assume they know telecom or NBFC)

Give a pitch script (keep it natural, not robotic)

Share do's & don'ts (e.g. don't sit on the canopy table!)

Dress code & grooming (branded T shirt or neat formal wear)

Pitch Example for NBFC Gold Loan:

> "Sir, we're offering instant gold loans with 0 processing fees. Can I help you check eligibility in 2 mins?"

🔒 Pro Tip: Run a 15 min roleplay at start of the day. You'll thank yourself later.

## ⏱ 3. Daily Execution Flow

| Time | Task |
|---|---|
| 8.30 AM | Team assembly + setup |
| 9.00 AM | Branding installed + dry run |
| 10.00 AM TO 12.00 PM | Public starts engaging |
| 1.00 PM | Break rotation (never leave stall empty) |
| 2.00 PM | Mid-day check: leads collected so far |
| 5.00 PM | Peak footfall – full team alert |
| 7.00 PM | Wrap up + count flyers/leads |
| 7.30 PM | Feedback sent to HO/you |

🔒 Pro Tip: Take short videos/pics every 3 hours. Helps in reporting, proof, and learning.

## 4. Lead Capturing: Go Digital if You Can

Forget paper forms if you can avoid it. They get wet, torn, or lost.

Better Options:

Google Form with name/number/location

QR code to open app/install form

WhatsApp opt in (promoter sends message and gets reply)

Tablet form with Airtable/JotForm

🔒 Pro Tip: Use numbering to track how many people filled forms. E.g., Form No. 47 = 47th lead today.

## 5. Common Problems in the Field (And Fixes)

| Issue | Fix |
|---|---|
| Promoter not showing up | Keep 1 standby promoter always available |
| Rain/wind damage setup | Carry plastic sheets + weighted stands |
| Police asking to shut down | Show permission letter (or shift to private spot) |
| Public ignoring you | Try candy/sample/quiz to initiate conversations |
| Tech not working (QR/code) | Keep backup printed forms |
| Low energy team | Run hourly incentives: "5 leads in 30 mins = ₹100" |

## 6. Real Case: FMCG Sampling in Chennai Mall

> 3 promoters + 1 floor managers

> Distributed 2,000 sachets in 2 days

> Trick: Gave a "Rate Us" card with smiley/frowny faces → 80% positive

> Bonus: Got 110 Insta tags via selfie contest

🔒 Pro Tip: Gamify boring campaigns— "Spin the wheel" or "Lucky dip" attracts crowds fast.

# 7. Reporting at Day End

Always submit a  simple daily tracker.

Sample Format:

```

Location: Phoenix Market city, Pune

Date: 8 June 2025

Footfall: 3,200

Interactions: 1,500

Leads: 420

App Installs: 180

Attachments: 4 photos, 1 promoter video

Issues: Rain 2–3 PM, team resumed by 3:15

Feedback: Students were most interested. Try college fest next.

Pro Tip:  Use voice notes if you're too tired. Just keep it daily.

### Field Execution Tips from Pros

> "I always carry two extra banners. One always falls or fades."

> Hari, BTL Lead, Telecom Brand

> "Don't underestimate local tea shop near stall. That guy sends you walk ins if you chat with him."

> Nita, FMCG Field Head

> "Power bank is a life saver when you're running QR codes all day."

> Rahul, Retail BTL Executive
```

## Chapter 10: Creativity in BTL – When Small Budgets Create Big Magic

You don't need money to be memorable. Just guts, ideas, and execution.

### Why This Chapter Matters

Your first BTL campaign probably won't have LED vans or drones. But guess what?

A well-timed WhatsApp challenge or a ₹50 spinning wheel can outperform  a ₹5L hoarding.

Creativity is your  ROI multiplier.

### 1. What Makes a BTL Idea "Creative"?

☑ Grabs attention

☑ Easy to participate

☑ Feels local and personal

☑ Gets people talking (or sharing)

☑ Costs little but does a lot

The goal?  Turn heads + generate leads.

## ⚡ 2. Killer Low-Cost Creative Ideas by Sector

### ⊚ NBFC (Gold Loans, Personal Loans)

| Idea | Description |
|---|---|
| Gold Drop Challenge | Weigh your bag > get free gift if over 1kg (symbolic) |
| Spin & Win EMI Game | QR scan to spin a virtual wheel with small prizes |
| "Bring Your Gold" Selfie | Get a selfie at stall → Win a voucher |
| Local Story Wall | Customers write why they took a gold loan → Best wins |

### 📶 Telecom

| Idea | Description |
|---|---|
| Speed Test Booth | Show how your SIM beats others in speed live |
| Chai on Us | Free tea for SIM switchers → informal lead gen |
| Data Plan Jenga | Jenga tower with plan cards—pull one & get free data |

### 🧴 FMCG

| Idea | Description |
|---|---|
| Smell Challenge | Blindfold test of your brand vs others |
| Fresh Face Selfie Spot | Mirror + frame→ Upload with brand hashtag |
| Lucky Sample Pack | One sample out of 10 contains a "golden card" win |

### 🛍 Retail

| Idea | Description |
|---|---|
| Drop a Bill Contest | Show any old bill > Get instant scratch card |
| QR Code Treasure Hunt | Scan codes across store, solve clues, get discount |
| Customer of the Hour | Loudly announce and award random visitor |

🔖 Pro Tip: Tie  every activity back to data capture.  That's your true win.

## 3. WhatsApp & QR Code – Your Secret Creative Weapons

### WhatsApp Campaign Ideas:

Voice Note Quiz: Ask 3 questions via audio → best replies get a reward

Story Stickers: Customers use your brand sticker on their Status

Referral Chain: "Forward to 5 friends and show us replies to win"

### QR Code Smart Hacks:

Use it to open a game, form, or lucky draw

Redirect to Insta Reel with product demo

Link to branch/store Google Maps with offer

Generate dynamic coupon code

🔒 Pro Tip: Use Bitly + QR Tiger for custom QR codes that track scans.

### 4. College Fest & Local Event Hacks

Colleges are GOLD for BTL. Why?

High energy

Social media active

Open to fun interactions

What You Can Do:

| Idea | Impact |
|---|---|
| Selfie Booth + Hashtag | Tag + post = win |
| Scream Contest | Who shouts brand slogan loudest wins |
| Speed Trials (FMCG) | Use + rate your product in 10 seconds |
| Referral Stickers | "Ask me about gold loans" – winner = most leads |

🔒 Pro Tip: Give the college union head a freebie or internship referral—they'll push it for you.

### 5. Real Case: Telecom Brand's QR Surprise

> Campaign: "QR for Recharge"

> Strategy: Flyers with QR code leading to a mystery gift page

> Result: 8,700 scans in 6 days, 1,600 SIM activations, ₹1.2L spend

> Learning: 80% scans came in 1st 2 days—create urgency!

### 6. The Magic Formula: Simple + Local + Fun

Simple: No app install, no long forms

Local: Add the city name, language, or local face

Fun: Make people laugh, guess, shout, pose

Example:

> "Chechi Challenge: Can you say our loan slogan in Malayalam faster than our promoter? Win a ₹50 Amazon gift."

🔒 Pro Tip: Make activities camera friendly —Reels, selfies, funny clips. Visibility = virality.

### 7. Prize Ideas Under ₹50

| Prize | Notes |
|---|---|
| Free recharge | Popular for youth/Tier 3 |
| Scratch card | Hidden excitement |
| Candy + referral card | Great for retail footfall |
| Instant coffee packs | Easy FMCG tie ins |
| Brand badge/sticker | Helps social sharing |
| ₹20 coupon | Digital QR based redemption |

🔒 Pro Tip: Always over order gifts by 10%. Nothing kills momentum like "Oops, gift over."

☑ Final Tip: Creativity > Budget

> "My ₹18,000 selfie frame stall got me 300 leads.

> My ₹2L roadshow van got me 90 leads."

> — Meera, Junior BTL Manager, FMCG Brand

You don't need big money to win in BTL.

You need big energy, a few bold ideas, and execution that makes people stop and smile.

# Chapter 11: BTL x Digital – Blending Offline Hustle with Online Muscle

The best BTL campaigns don't end in the streets—they go viral online.

### 💡 Why This Chapter Matters

BTL is physical. But   your audience lives on their phones.

Mix the two and you can:

Boost reach

Collect better data

Retarget warm leads

Track real time impact

Let's bridge the gap between   the promoter and the pixel.

### 🔗 1. Why BTL Needs Digital Now

| BTL Alone | BTL + Digital |
|---|---|
| One time visibility | Ongoing engagement |
| Manual lead capture | Instant form entry / CRM sync |
| Local reach | Hyperlocal + Online reach |
| Hard to measure ROI | Clicks, scans, shares = real data |

🎯 Truth Bomb: If no one clicks, shares or comments, your campaign is invisible beyond the street.

## ⚙ 2. Plug & Play Digital Add Ons

### ▦ WhatsApp

Auto replies ("Thanks for visiting our stall, here's your coupon!")

Group creation for follow up or contest winners

Feedback collection via chat

### ▣ Instagram

Story filter branded challenge

Reel contest with hashtags

Selfie zone uploads + tagging

### ▤ Google Forms / Typeform

Instant lead capture

Route to CRM

Automate thank you emails/SMS

### ⊕ Landing Pages / Microsites

For special offers (e.g., telco plans)

Track traffic from QR codes

Collect contact + consent

## ◎ 3. Funnel Your Footfalls – The BTL to CRM Flow

1.  Customer visits canopy

2. Promoter collects info via QR scan (Form)

3. Data syncs with CRM or Google Sheet

4. Lead scoring by quality (ex: location match, intent)

5. Automated SMS → "Hey Ramesh, thanks for stopping by!"

🔒 Pro Tip: Add tags like "BTL\_City Mall" so you can track source of conversion later.

## 4. Measurement Magic – Go Beyond "Leads"

Here's what smart BTL x Digital teams measure:

| Metric | Why It Matters |
|---|---|
| Form fill count | Lead volume |
| QR code scans | Engagement strength |
| Social media mentions | Organic buzz |
| Redemption rate (e.g. coupon) | Conversion |
| Time on page (microsite) | Interest quality |
| Bounce rate | Did people leave immediately? |

🔖 Pro Tip: Use Bitly or UTM links to separate each location/stall's performance.

## 5. Campaign Example: NBFC Loan Drive

> Offline: Canopy set up near jewellery stores

> Online: QR scan → eligibility check → WhatsApp follow up

> Result:

> 2,100 scans

> 680 qualified leads

> 145 customers visited branch within 72 hrs

> ₹23L disbursed in 5 days

🔖 Bonus Hack: Create a digital scratch card via website – people LOVE gamified coupons.

## 6. Viral Loops – How to Make Your BTL Campaign Travel

Ideas that Spread:

Contest with share to win

"Tag a friend who..." type prompts

QR scan > Instagram filter > post

Spin the wheel web page (share to unlock)

Example: FMCG brand gave free shampoo samples at railway stations. Every sample had a QR that opened a filter → share = entry into ₹100 Amazon contest.

5,000+ shares, ₹12,000 total spend.

## 7. Must Have Tools for BTL x Digital

| Tool | Use |
|------|-----|
| Canva / Mojo | Insta reel & story content |
| Bitly | Trackable QR links |
| Jotform / Typeform | Stylish forms |
| WhatsApp Business | Auto messaging, catalogue |
| Google Sheets + Zapier | CRM like tracking & alerts |
| Mailchimp / SMS tools | Nurture via drip campaigns |

Pro Tip: Use "Zaps" to auto add lead entries to your CRM and shoot SMS on the spot.

## 8. What Experts Say

> "We stopped paper forms after one festival. WhatsApp form got us cleaner data and 60% more follow ups."

> — Akshay, Retail BTL Manager

> "Our Loan Challenge reel got only 6 leads but 40K views. Two competitors even copied it."

> — Priya, NBFC Campaign Lead

> "Don't wait to digitize BTL. Customers expect a quick scan, not a 5 min talk."

> — Nilesh, Telecom Zonal Head

💡 Final Thoughts

🔁 BTL without digital = one time burst

⚡ BTL with digital = trackable, repeatable, scalable impact

The future is  phygital (physical + digital).

# Chapter 12: Getting Started – How to Launch Your First BTL Campaign

You've got the ideas. Now let's hit the road.

🔦 Why This Chapter Matters

You're new. You're energetic. But you're also wondering:

Where do I begin?

What if the campaign flops?

What does a good BTL launch look like?

This chapter is your step-by-step launch kit.

📖 1. 15 Step Launch Timeline (3 Weeks to D Day)

| Day | Task |
|---|---|
| D - 21 | Finalize product/offer focus (get buy in from sales/branch teams) |
| D - 19 | Choose target audience + location (e.g., college, market, rural fair) |
| D - 17 | Budget approval (₹15K to ₹3L typical range) |
| D - 15 | Design creatives (flyers, banners, QR code forms) |
| D - 14 | Vendor finalization (promoters, printing, canopy/tent) |
| D - 12 | Create lead form, QR, WhatsApp workflow |
| D - 10 | Field visit or recce + permission paperwork |
| D - 8 | Order material printing + finalize incentive plan |
| D - 5 | Team briefing (promoters, SPOC, supervisors) |
| D - 3 | Dry run / test form & QR with real user |
| D - 1 | Setup delivery, pack up kit, team motivation call |
| D | Launch with energy, track every hour, click photos |
| D 1 | Debrief + report with learnings |
| D 3 | Data handover to sales/branch |
| D 7 | Follow up report on conversion + feedback |

🔒 Pro Tip: Keep a simple project tracker in Excel or Google Sheets.

## 2. Sample BTL Campaign Budget (₹40,000 Example – NBFC)

| Item | Cost Estimate |
|---|---|
| Canopy + setup | ₹ 6,000 |
| Branding & print | ₹ 5,000 |
| Promoters (2 x 3 days) | ₹ 9,000 |
| Gifts & coupons | ₹ 5,000 |
| Travel/logistics | ₹ 3,000 |
| QR/Forms setup | ₹ 1,000 |
| Snacks + water | ₹ 1,000 |
| Contingency (10%) | ₹ 4,000 |
| **Total** | **₹34,000–₹40,000** |

🔒 Pro Tip: If tight on budget, skip canopy—just do a "walking BTL" with branded t shirts and QR flyers.

## 3. The Launch Team – Who Does What

| Role | Responsibility |
|---|---|
| Campaign Lead | You—owner of everything |
| Designer | Creatives for print & digital |
| Vendor | Prints + installs + promoter arrangement |
| Branch Head | Local support & conversion follow up |
| Promoters | Field engagement |
| Data SPOC | CRM entry or sheet tracking |

🔒 Pro Tip: Never run BTL alone—always have 1 field partner or manager.

## 4. What to Pack for the Field

2 Printed banners

50 flyers/day

Promoter pitch script

Power bank + backup sim

First aid kit

Snacks + water

Google Form shortlink + QR printed

₹ change for cash-based gifts

Bluetooth speaker (music draws crowds!)

🔒 Pro Tip: Keep digital copy of permissions and pitch deck on your phone.

## 5. Reporting Template

Send within 12 hours post activity.

📍 Location: M.G. Road, Kochi

📅 Date: 10 June 2025

🧍 Promoters: 2

👥 Footfall: 2,000 approx.

📝 Leads: 412

📞 Qualified Leads: 155

🔁 Repeat Questions: "How much gold do I need?" "Is CIBIL needed?"

📷 Photos: 4 attached

🎯 Insights: Target women in evening shift (4–7PM is gold!)

⚡ Issues: No power plug, had to use power bank.

✅ Follow up: Shared data with Kochi branch, next camp planned.

🔒 **Pro Tip:** Share 1 killer photo + quote from a customer. Looks great in decks.

## 6. Tips for New Executives

**Start small, scale fast** – Run a pilot in 1 mall, learn, repeat in 5 cities.

**Build a local network** – Know the best promoters, print shops, and food vendors.

**Speak the field language** – Respect the field team's pace and effort.

**Always carry Plan B** – BTL = chaos. Have backups for everything.

**Show numbers, not just effort** – Leads, scans, redemptions > "worked hard"

🔒 **Pro Tip:** Your first BTL campaign will be messy—and unforgettable. Own it.

# Chapter 13: Vendor Management – Your Secret Weapon in BTL

Vendors are the lifeblood of BTL execution. Whether it's printing danglers, deploying promoters, or setting up stalls at a local fair — your vendor network can make or break a campaign.

This chapter will help you:

- Identify key vendor types
- Set expectations clearly
- Avoid common mistakes
- Track and rate performance
- Handle vendor payments and delays

## ✅ BTL Vendor Rating Sheet (Post-Campaign)

| Vendor Name | Service Provided | Cost (₹) | Timeliness (1-5) | Quality (1-5) | Communication (1-5) | Flexibility (1-5) | Overall Score | Notes/ Remarks |
|---|---|---|---|---|---|---|---|---|
|  |  |  |  |  |  |  |  |  |
|  |  |  |  |  |  |  |  |  |
|  |  |  |  |  |  |  |  |  |

Scoring Guide:
- 1 = Poor, 3 = Average, 5 = Excellent
- Overall Score = Average of the 4 rating columns

## ◈ Vendor Payment Tracker

| Vendor Name | Service Provided | Invoice No. | Amount (₹) | Payment Status | Payment Date |
|---|---|---|---|---|---|
|  |  |  |  |  |  |
|  |  |  |  |  |  |

## ✳ Handling Vendor Payment Delays

- Always maintain a clear email trail with invoice dates and approval timelines.
- Set expectations about TAT (turnaround time) for payments at the time of briefing.
- Create a vendor agreement with penalty clauses for non-performance, but also mention payment windows.
- Follow up formally — weekly email reminders + shared tracker works well.
- Escalate diplomatically if needed, especially in larger organizations.

## 🔍 Identifying Vendor Needs

Before you bring a vendor on board, be clear about what you need. Here is how:

- Break down the campaign: What parts will need external help? (Printing, logistics, manpower, permits?)
- Define deliverables: Quantity, quality, timeline, and location specifics.
- Match vendors to roles: Don't hire a printer for event fabrication. Specialization matters.
- Evaluate based on: Experience in your industry, geographic familiarity, ability to scale.

Pro Tip: Don't wait until the last minute. Start scouting vendors the moment your plan is sketched.

## Mastering Vendor Negotiation

Negotiation isn't about haggling—it's about ensuring mutual value. Here is a quick playbook:

1. Know the market  – Benchmark prices from previous campaigns or peers.
2. Get multiple quotes  – At least 2–3 to compare value, not just cost.
3. Bundle deliverables  – Offer multiple items or repeat work to get volume discounts.
4. Ask for breakdowns  – Material, manpower, transport. It helps you negotiate line by line.
5. Insist on timelines  – With clear milestones tied to payments.
6. Quality clauses  – Always insert quality benchmarks to avoid poor output.

Tip: Be polite but firm. Good negotiation is professional and respectful. Vendors are partners, not adversaries.

# ⊚ Chapter 14: Budgeting & Cost Control in BTL

BTL campaigns often look flashy and spontaneous on the outside —
but behind every successful ground activation is a marketer juggling
spreadsheets, vendor calls, and last-minute cost cuts. Let's break
down how to budget smartly and squeeze the most value from every
rupee.

### ⚑ Why Budgeting Matters in BTL

Unlike ATL media with standard rate cards, BTL campaigns vary
dramatically based on:

Location (urban vs rural),

Time (festive seasons are expensive),

Format (a kiosk in a mall costs more than a shop front canopy).

Without clear budgeting:

You'll overspend early and have to cut corners at the end.

Vendor negotiations will be vague and inflated.

ROI tracking becomes a guessing game.

### ◈ Common BTL Budget Heads

| Cost Head | What It Covers |
|---|---|
| Manpower | Promoters, supervisors, field coordinators |
| Logistics | Travel, freight, set-up/dismantle transport |
| Fabrication | Canopies, stalls, kiosks, banners, cut-outs |
| Printing | Leaflets, danglers, posters, standees |
| Permissions | Mall entry, local police/NOC, shop association fees |
| Sampling Stock | Product units (if not supplied by brand) |
| Contingency | Weather-related backups, rush printing |
| Agency Fee | Handling and coordination costs (usually 10–15%) |

# How to Create a Campaign Budget (Step-by-Step)

1. Start with the Brief

   Objective: Awareness / Conversion / Footfall?

   Duration: One day / Week / Month?

   Geography: One city or pan-India?

2. List Activities

   E.g., Canopy at 50 retail outlets across 2 cities for 7 days

3. Break Down Each Activity

   Manpower: ₹1,200/day × 7 days × 50 = ₹4.2L

   Printing: 2,000 leaflets × ₹2 = ₹4,000

   Setup: Stall per outlet = ₹800 × 50 = ₹40,000

4. Factor in Vendor Margins + Hidden Costs

   Always assume 5–10% fluctuation for fuel, permit changes, etc.

5. Set a Cap for Each Head

   Helps avoid panic approvals mid-campaign

   ✗ Tools to Use (Simple Works Best)

   Google Sheets   for team collaboration and live updates

   Excel   with filters & auto-formulas for per-unit cost analysis

   Track per activity, per vendor, and include "Actual vs Estimated" columns for learning

## 🔍 Cost Control Hacks (Without Sacrificing Impact)

Bundle vendors   across geographies to get better rates

Centralize printing in bulk — cheaper than local last-minute jobs,
Always look out for hub level stocking.

Use digital wherever possible  — QR codes instead of printed
coupons

Rent instead of build  — reusable booths/stalls save cost over time,
Build only if long term re use is there.

Train promoters in-house  if it's a long-term campaign

## ✏️ Mini Case Study: Cost-Effective Retail Blitz

Scenario:  FMCG brand needed a 10-day visibility and sampling
campaign across 30 stores in Tier 2 towns. Initial budget: ₹3.2L

Smart Hacks Used:

Shared one fabrication partner for all booths (bulk rate ₹500 per
stall)

Used digital feedback instead of paper coupons

Trained 3 in-house interns as backup promoters

Final Spend:  ₹2.26L

Leads Generated:  1,450

Cost Per Lead:  ₹156

## ■ MATERIAL SPECIFICATIONS TO INSIST ON

Vendors often cut corners on print and fabrication unless you're specific. Here's a quick spec sheet for common BTL items:

| Material Type | Specification | Notes |
|---|---|---|
| Leaflets | 80 GSM Maplitho Paper, A5 size | Use 4-color print for branding clarity |
| Posters | 100–130 GSM Art Paper, A3 size | Ideal for indoor visibility |
| Flex Banners | Indian Flex or Star Flex, 13 oz thickness | Star Flex is better for longer campaigns |
| Standees | Vinyl Print on Eco-solvent with 3mm Sunboard backing | Use SS pipes for stability |
| Canopy Booths | MS Square Pipe Frame (22 Gauge), Sunpack walls/MDF | Avoid bamboo or plastic for multi-day use |
| Promoter T-Shirts | 180–200 GSM Cotton with 2-color screen printing or embroidery | Include brand logo + campaign hashtag |
| Backdrops | 280 GSM Cloth Print or Star Flex on metal stand | Windproof stitching recommended for outdoors |
| QR Code Posters | 250 GSM Art Card with lamination | Prevents fading/tearing during campaign runtime |
| Counters/Tables | 10mm MDF with vinyl branding wrap | Prefer collapsible/foldable formats for transport ease |

# ✉ Chapter 15: How to Brief an Agency or Vendor

Your brief is your blueprint. Whether you're setting up a mall activation or a rural van campaign, how well you brief your vendor or agency will determine execution quality, budget accuracy, and turnaround time. A good brief saves you from dozens of back-and-forth calls and "this wasn't told earlier" excuses.

## 💬 First, What Is a Good Brief?

A good brief:

Clarifies the objective   (Branding? Sampling? Leads?)

Defines the target group   (Age, income, location, lifestyle)

Details the deliverables   (Qty, size, placement, frequency)

Mentions budget band   (So agencies propose within range)

Shares timelines & approvals process

Lists key KPIs   for success measurement

## 📋 Sample Brief Format

You don't need a fancy template. Even a well-structured email or shared doc can work. Here's a go-to format:

| Section | Details to Include |
|---|---|
| Objective | What are we trying to achieve? (e.g., awareness, trials, leads, walk-ins) |
| Target Audience (TG) | Who are we speaking to? (age group, income class, urban/rural, interests) |
| Geography | Cities, districts, pin codes to be covered |
| Duration | Campaign start & end dates |
| Deliverables | No. of stalls, flex size, flyer count, branding units, promoter count, etc. |
| Creative Direction | Brand colors, taglines, imagery references |
| Budget Band | E.g., ₹4.5L to ₹5L — gives flexibility for scope ideas |
| Key Metrics/KPIs | Leads, footfall, sampling count, video/photo coverage |
| Stakeholders & Roles | Who approves creatives, timelines, and who's the final decision maker? |

☑ Share samples of past campaigns, if available — visuals help vendors get aligned faster.

### ○ Why Vendors Mis-interpret Briefs (And How to Avoid It)

Vague words  like "massive" or "high footfall" — use numbers instead (e.g., "target: 300 people/day")

Assumed knowledge  — always explain local context, even if you've worked together before

Last-minute changes  — brief should be frozen before fabrication or deployment starts

✳ Tip:  Have a kickoff call after sharing the brief to walk vendors through it. Record the call and share notes to avoid future confusion.

### ✕ Briefing Tools That Work

Google Docs  for real-time editable briefs

WhatsApp groups  for urgent clarifications (but don't brief only on chat!)

PDF or PPT  if visuals are important (layout, stall design, etc.)

## ◎ Real-Life Example

Brief Title:  Rural Sampling + Awareness for New Packaged Drink

Location:  Tamil Nadu - Tier 3 towns

Deliverables:

10 promoters for 3 days

5 branded tables

20K leaflets

10 standees

Live announcements via PA system

Objective:  Sampling + Audio engagement

KPI:  Reach 10,000 people & distribute 7,000 samples

◆ Because the brief was clear, the agency delivered under budget and on time. The client renewed the campaign in 3 more states.

# 🔔 Chapter 16: Handling Crisis On-Ground

No matter how well you plan, things will go wrong. Welcome to BTL marketing — where rains, riots, manpower issues, and even cows on the road can derail your day. The goal isn't to avoid crisis completely — it's to stay ready and bounce back fast.

Common BTL Crises (and What to Do)

| Crisis | Response |
|---|---|
| Promoter doesn't show up | Always keep backup promoters on roster or standby |
| Rain or wind damage the setup | Use waterproof flex, sandbags, and emergency plastic covers |
| Local permission not received | Carry printed email trails, get alternate spots pre-approved |
| Collateral not delivered on time | Keep a stash of general-purpose stock (leaflets, danglers) at the base |
| Technical glitch (mic, tablet fails) | Keep spares, and always test setup before event begins |
| Crowd trouble / aggressive TG | Train promoters in basic conflict resolution, have security if needed |

☑ Create a BTL Emergency Kit

Just like doctors have a medical bag, BTL marketers need a go-to kit. Here's what it should include:

Rain covers   (plastic sheets, flex jackets)

Extra flex ties & hooks

Scissors, cutter, masking tape

Basic first-aid kit

Power bank, extension cords

Offline brand guidelines on a pen drive or phone

◆ Pro Tip: Keep copies of IDs, permissions, invoices — both printed and digital — in case of spot checks.

### ▦ Real-Time Troubleshooting Channels

WhatsApp groups:  Add all key stakeholders — your team, vendor lead, promoter agency, client coordinator

Google Drive:  Upload all designs, collaterals, IDs, permits — easy to reprint in emergencies

Geo-tag photos:  Every site report should include timestamped geo-tagged photos

### 💬 Soft Skills That Help During Crisis

Stay calm  — field teams take cues from your tone

Listen before reacting  — don't jump to blame

Take ownership with the client  — then troubleshoot internally

Be decisive  — 10 seconds of silence can cost a crowd

### 📖 Real Crisis Story: Kerala Hartal

During a mall activation in Kochi, we had 3 promoters pull out due to a sudden local hartal. Roads were blocked, and crowd traffic was thin.

What we did:

Shifted the setup 200m into a safe zone inside the mall complex

Re-deployed 2 standby interns trained earlier

Activated social media posts to drive audience into the location

✦ Result: We salvaged 70% of the campaign target footfall with minor disruption — and won client trust for smart handling.

Would you like this added to the Word file and then move to  Bonus Chapter 4: Measuring Success Beyond ROI ?

Absolutely! A **field-ready event checklist** is essential for young marketers to manage on-ground execution confidently — and stay prepared for emergencies.

## 📋 BTL Event Execution & Crisis Management Checklist

Use this list 2–3 days **before the event, on the event day**, and **post-event** to ensure everything runs smoothly.

| ☑ PRE-EVENT CHECKLIST (2–3 Days Before) | | |
|---|---|---|
| **Task** | **Status** | **Notes** |
| Vendor finalization & POs released | ☐ | Confirm all commercial terms |
| Collateral print-ready & approved | ☐ | Banners, leaflets, standees, etc. |
| Manpower confirmed with agency | ☐ | Names, IDs, shift timing |
| Permissions in place (mall/local) | ☐ | Soft copy + hard copy in event file |
| Route plans/venue maps received | ☐ | Check entry, power points |
| Event WhatsApp group created | ☐ | Add all key stakeholders |
| Backup promoters/interns prepped | ☐ | At least 1 backup for every 3-5 people |
| Weather checked + cover plan ready | ☐ | Plastic sheets / alternate venue |
| Brand kits (t-shirts, IDs, etc.) | ☐ | Neatly packed, one per promoter |

| ☑ ON-DAY CHECKLIST | | |
|---|---|---|
| **Task** | **Status** | **Notes** |
| Setup done before time | ☐ | Allow 90 mins buffer |
| All collaterals in place | ☐ | As per branding guide |
| Promoters in uniform + trained | ☐ | Last-minute briefing to be done |
| Crowd control/security briefed | ☐ | Required for high-footfall events |
| Event photos & videos taken | ☐ | Capture setup, crowd, interaction |
| Checklists signed by ground lead | ☐ | Capture time-in/time-out |

| ⊡ CRISIS BACKUP ITEMS CHECKLIST | | |
|---|---|---|
| **Backup Item** | **Status** | **Notes** |
| Extra Flex & Zip Ties | ☐ | At least 1 spare for every key banner |
| Printed Permissions/Letters | ☐ | Carry printouts in plastic folder |
| First-Aid Kit | ☐ | Band-aids, antiseptic, pain relief |
| Plastic Covers (for rain) | ☐ | One roll per stall |
| Phone Charging Power Bank | ☐ | Fully charged, with cable |
| Offline Creative Files (USB) | ☐ | Includes logos, leaflets, standees |
| Emergency Numbers Printed | ☐ | Vendor, police, electrician |
| Extra T-shirts for Promoters | ☐ | For last-minute replacements |

| ⌦ POST-EVENT CHECKLIST | | |
|---|---|---|
| **Task** | **Status** | **Notes** |
| Collateral count verified | ☐ | What was used vs. leftover |
| Payments tracker updated | ☐ | Share with finance |
| Photos/videos uploaded | ☐ | Google Drive folder shared |
| Client report sent | ☐ | With metrics & event summary |
| Debrief with vendor/team done | ☐ | Lessons, errors, feedback noted |

# Chapter 17: Measuring Success Beyond ROI

A flex was printed. A booth was set up. Some photos were taken. Everyone went home.

✅ But was that really a successful BTL activity?

Here's the truth: BTL isn't a checklist. It's a business tool.

If your activity doesn't move the needle — in brand recall, lead flow, or customer behaviour — it's just noise.

## 🔋 BTL is NOT a Tick Mark Task

Many campaigns go live only to "show presence" or "because the budget was approved." That's dangerous. It leads to:

Wasted money

Burnt out teams

Zero real returns

💧 Every BTL activity must answer this: "What business outcome did this generate?"

Whether it's leads, store visits, sampling conversions, or social media buzz — your setup should spark action .

## 💬 3 Levels of Success to Track

| Level | What to Measure | Why It Matters |
|---|---|---|
| 1 Basic ROI | Leads, walk ins, redemptions | Shows if spend = returns |
| 2 Engagement | Interactions, dwell time, questions asked | Shows if the TG actually cared and influence |
| 3 Brand Uplift | Recall, social shares, feedback, loyalty | Shows long term memory, trust, |

## Key Metrics That Matter (More Than Just ROI)

| Metric | Description | Track Using |
|---|---|---|
| Footfall | How many people noticed or engaged with you? | Manual count / footfall sensors |
| Dwell Time | Did people stop or just walk past? | Stopwatch, video playback |
| Sampling Conversion % | Tried product ÷Total visitors | Promoter records |
| Leads Captured | Total inquiries or form fills | Digital lead forms / CRM |
| Feedback Quality | Real user thoughts on product/experience | Google Forms, live surveys |
| Repeat Visits / Actions | Did anyone comeback or engage again later? | CRM / QR analytics |

## Digital Tools You Can Use

QR Code landing pages → Drive users to sign up or rate the experience

Photo booths/selfie spots → Drive social sharing, track impressions

NPS or Emoji Stations → Capture sentiment instantly

### Stop Doing This:

Just printing 5000 leaflets without distribution tracking

Running a booth with no footfall goals or lead forms

Collecting data and doing nothing with it

Reporting success as "activity completed" instead of "impact created"

☑ Do This Instead:

Align every activity with a  clear KPI  (e.g., "We aim to generate 300 leads in 3 days")

Set a  benchmark  before and after (e.g., store footfall, product trials)

Always link activation to a  business goal  (awareness, acquisition, loyalty)

▨ Case Study: Telecom SIM Exchange Drive

Objective:  Switch customers from competitor networks

Method:  Setup at recharge shops + incentive for switching

Result:

1100 SIM port ins in 4 days

90% of activations done on site

3x ROI from local brand visibility via banners

➤ They didn't just show up. They  converted .

◯ Field Quote

"Don't run a campaign because 'everyone's doing it.' Run it because you can prove it works — even on a small scale."

Field Marketing Manager, NBFC

# Chapter 18: Roadshows that Deliver

A roadshow isn't just a moving billboard. Done right, it's a mobile engagement engine — driving visibility, footfalls, and solid leads across regions.

## 🚐 WHY ROADSHOWS WORK
- They go *to* the customer — perfect for semi-urban, rural, and spread-out markets.
- They mix awareness with direct lead-gen (especially useful for NBFC, telecom, and FMCG).
- Create local buzz and improve recall if executed with consistency.

## 🚌 THE ROUTE PLAN IS EVERYTHING
- Finalize route 3–4 days in advance — mix high-footfall + hyperlocal spots.
- Share route with all stakeholders: client, agency, ops team, local branches.
- Include fuel stop points, safe parking zones, and local landmarks for promoter pick-up.

## 💼 ROADSHOW KIT CHECKLIST
- Branded van with sound and mic system
- Flex drops or canopies for high-traffic points
- Promoter IDs, uniforms, and brand kit
- Brochures/leaflets + sampling items (if any)
- Lead forms (digital preferred)
- GPS/mileage tracking system or manual logbook
- First aid + backup fuel + roadside tools

## 🎯 DECIDE YOUR ENGAGEMENT HOOK
- Fun games like spin-the-wheel or scratch-and-win
- Product demos or quick challenges (e.g., speed puzzle)
- Lucky draws or QR code-based instant rewards
- Ask-me-anything booths for NBFC, telecom FAQs

## 📝 DAILY TRACKER FORMAT

| Date | Location | Leads Collected | Distance Covered (KM) | Local Branch Contact | Photos Shared |
|------|----------|-----------------|-----------------------|----------------------|---------------|
|      |          |                 |                       |                      |               |

Track mileage honestly — it helps validate your reach and optimize routes next time.

## 📷 DAILY UPDATES PROTOCOL
- Every 2–3 hours: share WhatsApp photos with timestamp and location
- Use Google Drive folders for clean archiving
- End-of-day summary: locations visited, leads, issues faced

## 🤝 LOCAL TEAM INVOLVEMENT = BETTER RESULTS
- Loop in area branch heads well before rollout
- Ask them to join the roadshow when near their locality
- Provide real-time leads to local sales team — activate follow-ups in <24 hours
- Their presence builds brand trust locally and ensures conversion

*🖋 Remember: Roadshows are not parades. They're rolling campaigns. Every stop is an opportunity to engage, qualify, and convert.*

# 📋 Roadshow Van – Pre-Check & Launch Day Checklist

Before the roadshow hits the road, perform a thorough pre-check of the vehicle, branding quality, and logistics readiness. This ensures safety, durability, and a high-impact brand presence throughout.

## VEHICLE HEALTH CHECK

| Check Item | Status (☐/☑) | Remarks |
|---|---|---|
| Tyres (condition + spare) | ☐ | |
| Battery condition | ☐ | |
| Coolant, oil & brake fluid levels | ☐ | |
| Fuel tank full or planned top-up | ☐ | |
| Functioning headlights, indicators, horn, wipers | ☐ | |
| Road permit and PUC certificate available | ☐ | |

## BRANDING QUALITY CHECK

| Check Item | Status (☐/☑) | Remarks |
|---|---|---|
| Flex or vinyl wrap is wrinkle-free, properly mounted | ☐ | |
| Material used is weather-resistant (min 13oz star flex / vinyl) | ☐ | |
| Brand elements aligned, no pixelation or spelling errors | ☐ | |
| Side panels + rear properly covered and laminated (if needed) | ☐ | |
| All branding is clean, scratch-free, and uniform across vehicles | ☐ | |

## INTERIOR SETUP (IF APPLICABLE)

| Check Item | Status (☐/✅) | Remarks |
|---|---|---|
| Sample units secured (if displayed inside van) | ☐ | |
| Mic system and speakers tested | ☐ | |
| LED panels/screens are functional (if included) | ☐ | |
| Leaflet holders, product racks securely fixed | ☐ | |

## FLAG-OFF DAY READINESS

| Check Item | Status (☐/✅) | Remarks |
|---|---|---|
| Chief guest (if any) invited and confirmed | ☐ | |
| Van positioned for clean photo opportunity | ☐ | |
| Team in full uniform with ID cards | ☐ | |
| Ribbon/scissors, coconut/cracker (as per local custom) | ☐ | |
| Photographer/videographer ready to capture launch | ☐ | |
| Press/media (if planned) present or briefed | ☐ | |

# ✒ Chapter 19: Building a Career in BTL Marketing

BTL marketing may start with leaflets and promoter coordination, but it builds real-world skills that can take you all the way to the boardroom. If you love chaos, people, problem-solving, and quick wins — this is your playground.

Let's explore how to turn BTL into a long-term, rewarding career .

🐦 Why Start in BTL?

You learn faster — On-ground work teaches hustle, planning, people management

You develop thick skin — Dealing with promoters, vendors, clients prepares you for anything

You understand consumer behaviour firsthand — What ATL marketers guess from data, you see in real life

🔸 Many brand managers in FMCG, Telecom, and NBFC sectors started in BTL — they know what it's like to tape a flex at 6 am.

📈 Career Growth Path in BTL

Here's a realistic path for a fresher starting out in BTL or activation roles:

| Role | Years Exp | Skills to Master |
|---|---|---|
| BTL Executive | 0–2 | Coordination, field work, vendor follow-ups |
| Sr. Executive / Lead | 2–5 | Budgeting, briefing, reporting, team handling |
| Asst. Manager / Manager | 5–10 | Campaign strategy, agency mgmt, client presentations |
| Brand Activation Head | 10–15 | Cross-channel planning, ROI focus, innovation |
| Marketing Lead | 15+ | Integrated brand thinking, ATL + BTL + Digital |

## Skills You Must Build Early

Excel & Sheets : Budgeting, trackers, payments

PPT Design : Client reports, event decks, concepts

Vendor Negotiation : Costing, timelines, output quality

People Management : Promoters, interns, local staff

Crisis Handling : Confidence + clarity under pressure

Data Interpretation : Turning event data into insights

## Tools That Give You an Edge

Trello/Asana : Task & event tracking

Canva : Quick mockups and social content

Zapier/Google Forms : Automating data from promoters

CRM tools (Zoho/HubSpot) : To manage leads from events

## Voices from the Field

"I started by coordinating canopies in tier 3 towns — today I plan 360° campaigns for the brand."

Marketing Head, FMCG giant

"BTL taught me the value of 'Plan B' — it's the only place where Plan A almost never works."

Campaign Manager, Telecom brand

## Pro Tips for New Marketers

Don't skip the ground work — being present on-site is your best teacher

Document everything — photos, challenges, results — this becomes your portfolio

Speak to the consumer — once a week, face-to-face — it shapes your marketing instinct

## 🎉 YOU MADE IT!

From canopy to campaign report, from chai wala conversations to QR code dashboards— you now know what BTL marketing is really about.

Whether you're walking into your first brand event or planning a nation-wide street blitz— this playbook will keep you grounded and ready.

🔚 Final Wrap: Your BTL Survival Kit

Think like a local.

Plan like a pro.

Execute like a street-smart boss.

Report like a future CMO.

# GLOSSARY OF MARKETING TERMS AND ABBREVIATIONS

This comprehensive glossary provides definitions for key terms and abbreviations frequently encountered in the marketing domain, with a particular focus on concepts and practices relevant to Below-The-Line (BTL) marketing and Point-of-Sale (POS) materials.

# A

**A/B Testing:** A method of comparing two versions of a marketing asset (e.g., an ad, email, landing page) to determine which one performs better.

**Advergaming:** The practice of using video games to advertise a product, organization, or viewpoint.

**Advertising:** A marketing communication that employs an openly sponsored, non-personal message to promote or sell a product, service or idea.

**Affiliate Marketing:** A marketing arrangement in which an online retailer pays commission to an external website for traffic or sales generated from its referrals.

**AIDAS (Attention, Interest, Desire, Action, Satisfaction):** A classic marketing model outlining the stages a consumer goes through in the process of purchasing a product or service.

**Analytics:** The systematic computational analysis of data or statistics. In marketing, it refers to collecting, analyzing, and interpreting data to understand campaign performance.

**App Installs:** A metric tracking the number of times a mobile application is downloaded and installed by users, often a KPI for digital BTL.

**Activation:** A marketing activity designed to directly engage consumers with a brand, product, or service, often through interactive experiences, events, or demonstrations. (Primarily BTL)

**ATL (Above-The-Line):** Marketing activities that are broad in reach and untargeted, typically mass media campaigns like TV, radio, newspaper, and billboard advertising.

**Audience Segmentation:** The process of dividing a broad consumer or business market, normally consisting of existing and potential customers, into sub-groups of consumers (segments) based on some type of shared characteristics.

# B

**B2B (Business-to-Business):** Marketing efforts directed from one business to another.

**B2C (Business-to-Consumer):** Marketing efforts directed from a business to individual consumers.

**Banner Ad:** A form of advertising on the World Wide Web delivered by an ad server.

**Brand Ambassador:** A person employed by an organization or company to promote its products or services. (Often key in BTL)

**Brand Awareness:** The extent to which consumers are familiar with the distinctive qualities or image of a particular brand of goods or services.

**Brand Equity:** The commercial value that derives from consumer perception of the brand name of a particular product or service, rather than from the product or service itself.

**Brand Loyalty:** The tendency of consumers to continuously purchase one brand's products over competitors'.

**Brand Recall:** The ability of consumers to remember a brand name when prompted by a product category.

**Brand Visibility:** The degree to which a brand is noticeable or easily recognizable to its target audience in a given market or environment.

**Brief:** A document outlining the objectives, target audience, key messages, and requirements for a marketing campaign or creative project.

**Budgeting:** The process of estimating the financial resources required for a marketing campaign and allocating funds across various activities.

**BTL (Below-The-Line):** Marketing activities that are highly targeted, direct, and measurable, focusing on individual consumer engagement. Examples include direct mail, sales promotions, events, and in-store activations.

# C

**Call to Action (CTA):** An instruction to the audience designed to provoke an immediate response, such as "Buy Now," "Sign Up," or "Visit Our Store."

**Campaign:** A planned series of marketing activities designed to achieve a specific objective within a defined timeframe.

**Canopy:** A temporary, branded tent or shelter used for outdoor BTL activations and stalls.

**Channel Marketing:** Marketing efforts focused on promoting products through specific distribution channels (e.g., retail stores, distributors, online marketplaces).

**CIBIL (Credit Information Bureau (India) Limited):** A credit information company that maintains credit records of individuals and companies in India. (Relevant for NBFCs).

**Collaterals:** Marketing materials used to promote a product, brand, or service, such as flyers, brochures, posters, and standees.

**Content Marketing:** A strategic marketing approach focused on creating and distributing valuable, relevant, and consistent content to attract and retain a clearly defined audience.

**Conversion:** The point at which a recipient of a marketing message performs a desired action, such as making a purchase, signing up for a newsletter, or activating a SIM card.

**Conversion Rate:** The percentage of leads or interactions that result in a desired conversion.

**Copywriting:** The act or occupation of writing text for the purpose of advertising or other forms of marketing.

**Core Competencies:** The unique strengths and capabilities that give a company a competitive advantage.

**Cost Per Acquisition (CPA):** The total cost of a campaign divided by the number of conversions.

**Cost Per Click (CPC):** The amount an advertiser pays for each click on their advertisement.

**Cost Per Lead (CPL):** The total cost of a marketing campaign divided by the number of leads generated.

**CRM (Customer Relationship Management):** A system or strategy for managing a company's interactions with current and potential customers, often involving technology to organize, automate, and synchronize sales, marketing, customer service, and technical support.

**Customer Journey:** The complete sum of experiences that customers go through when interacting with a company or brand.

# D

**Data Analytics:** The science of examining raw data with the purpose of drawing conclusions about that information.

**Demographics:** Statistical data relating to the population and particular groups within it (e.g., age, gender, income, education).

**Digital Marketing:** The promotion of products or brands using electronic devices or the internet.

**Direct Mail:** Marketing material sent directly to consumers' homes or businesses via postal service. (BTL)

**Direct Marketing:** Marketing that relies on direct communication or distribution to individual consumers, rather than through a third party (like mass media). (BTL)

**Disbursement:** The act of paying out money, especially from a fund or loan. (Relevant for NBFCs).

**Display Advertising:** Visual advertisements that appear on websites, apps, or social media platforms.

# E

**E-commerce:** The buying and selling of goods or services using the internet.

**Email Marketing:** Sending commercial messages to a group of people using email.

**Engagement:** The level of interaction and involvement consumers have with a brand or marketing activity.

**Experiential Marketing:** A strategy that engages consumers through direct, memorable experiences, often involving events or interactive installations. (BTL)

**EPRS Channel (Exclusive Partner Retail Stores):** A specific type of retail channel, often exclusive to a brand or partner, focusing on direct sales and customer service.

# F

**Field Marketing:** Marketing activities conducted directly in the field, often involving personal interaction with consumers outside of traditional retail environments. (BTL)

**FMCG (Fast-Moving Consumer Goods):** Products that are sold quickly and at relatively low cost, such as packaged foods, beverages, toiletries, and over-the-counter drugs.

**Footfall:** The number of people entering a store or passing a specific location, often used as a metric for retail or event success.

**Freebie:** A complimentary item given away, often as part of a promotion or to attract engagement.

**Funnel (Marketing Funnel):** A visual representation of the customer journey, from initial awareness to conversion, typically narrowing at each stage.

# G

**Gamification:** The application of game-design elements and game principles in non-game contexts, often in marketing to increase engagement.

**Geotargeting:** Delivering content or advertising to a user based on their geographic location.

**Go-to-Market Strategy:** A comprehensive plan detailing how a company will bring a new product or service to market, including target audience, pricing, distribution, and marketing.

**Grassroots Marketing:** Marketing efforts that start at a local level, focusing on building relationships and word-of-mouth within a community. (BTL)

**Ground-Level Insights:** Practical, real-time observations and understandings gained directly from field operations or customer interactions.

# H

**Haats:** Traditional open-air markets, common in rural and semi-urban areas of India, often used for BTL activations.

**Hoarding:** A large outdoor advertising board; a billboard. (Primarily ATL, but BTL can refer to local, smaller hoardings).

**Hyperlocal:** Marketing efforts focused on a very specific, geographically limited area, often targeting consumers within a few miles of a business.

# I

**Impulse Purchase:** An unplanned decision to buy a product or service, often driven by immediate emotional response or in-store promotions.

**Influencer Marketing:** A form of marketing in which focus is placed on influential people rather than the target market as a whole.

**In-Store Branding:** Marketing materials and displays placed within a retail store to promote a product or brand at the point of sale. (BTL)

**ISD (In-Store Demonstrator/Sales Representative):** Personnel deployed within retail outlets to promote products, assist customers, and drive sales.

# K

**KPI (Key Performance Indicator):** A measurable value that demonstrates how effectively a company is achieving key business objectives.

**Kirana Store:** A small, local convenience store in India, often a key point for FMCG BTL activations.

# L

**Landing Page:** A standalone web page created specifically for a marketing or advertising campaign.

**Last-Mile Conversion:** The final step in the customer journey where a potential customer makes a purchase or completes a desired action, often influenced by in-store or direct marketing efforts.

**Lead Generation:** The process of identifying and cultivating potential customers for a business's products or services.

**Lead Nurturing:** The process of building relationships with prospects, even if they are not yet ready to buy, by providing relevant and valuable content.

**Leaflet:** A small, folded sheet of paper containing information or advertising, often distributed by hand. (BTL)

**Lifetime Value (LTV):** A prediction of the net profit attributed to the entire future relationship with a customer.

**Logistics:** The detailed organization and implementation of a complex operation, particularly the movement of materials, staff, and equipment for a campaign.

**Loyalty Program:** A rewards program offered by a company to customers who frequently make purchases.

# M

**Market Penetration:** The extent to which a product or brand is recognized and bought by customers in a particular market.

**Market Research:** The process of gathering, analyzing, and interpreting information about a market, about a product or service to be offered for sale in that market, and about the past, present and potential customers for the product or service.

**Marketing Mix (4 Ps):** Product, Price, Place, and Promotion – the foundational elements of a marketing strategy.

**Merchandising:** The promotion of goods and/or services that are available for retail sale, often through visual displays and product placement.

**Microsite:** A small, standalone website typically used for a specific marketing campaign, distinct from a company's main website.

**Microfinance:** A type of banking service provided to unemployed or low-income individuals or groups who otherwise have no access to financial services. (Relevant for NBFCs).

# N

**NBFC (Non-Banking Financial Company):** A company registered under the Companies Act that is engaged in the business of loans and advances, acquisition of shares/stocks/bonds/debentures/securities issued by government or local authority or other marketable securities of a like nature, leasing, hire-purchase, insurance business, chit business.

**NOC (No Objection Certificate):** A type of legal certificate issued by any agency, organization, or institute under certain circumstances. (Often required for BTL activations).

# P

**Phygital:** A term used to describe the blending of physical and digital experiences, creating a seamless interaction for consumers.

**Pilot:** A small-scale test of a campaign or activity before a full-scale rollout, used to identify potential issues and refine strategies.

**Pitch Card:** A small card containing key talking points or a script for promoters to use during direct interactions.

**POS (Point of Sale):**

The physical location where a transaction occurs, typically a retail store or counter.

Refers to **Point of Sale Materials (POSM)**: promotional materials used in retail environments to influence purchasing decisions at the point of purchase. (See detailed section below).

**Promoter:** An individual hired to directly engage with consumers, promote products, and often collect leads or drive sales at BTL activations.

**Promotional Mix:** The specific blend of advertising, public relations, personal selling, and sales promotion tools that a company uses to persuasively communicate customer value and build customer relationships.

**Psychographics:** The study and classification of people according to their attitudes, aspirations, and other psychological criteria.

**Public Relations (PR):** The practice of managing the spread of information between an individual or an organization and the public.

# Q

**QR Code (Quick Response Code):** A two-dimensional barcode readable by smartphones, used to link physical marketing materials to digital content (e.g., websites, forms, videos).

**Qualified Lead:** A lead that has been vetted and determined to have a high probability of becoming a customer.

# R

**Reach:** The total number of different people or households exposed to an advertisement or campaign at least once.

**Redemption:** The act of a customer claiming an offer, discount, or freebie, often by presenting a coupon or scanning a QR code.

**Retail Marketing:** Marketing activities specifically designed to attract customers to a retail store and encourage purchases.

**Roadshow:** A promotional event that travels to different locations, often using a branded vehicle, to engage with various audiences. (BTL)

**ROI (Return on Investment):** A performance measure used to evaluate the efficiency of an investment or compare the efficiency of several different investments. Calculated as (Gain from Investment - Cost of Investment) / Cost of Investment.

**RWA (Resident Welfare Association):** A body representing the residents of a particular residential area, often requiring permission for BTL activities within their jurisdiction.

# S

**Sales Promotion:** Short-term incentives to encourage the purchase or sale of a product or service. (BTL)

**Sampling:** The distribution of free product samples to consumers to encourage trial and purchase. (BTL)

**SEO (Search Engine Optimization):** The process of improving the visibility of a website or a web page in a search engine's unpaid results.

**SEM (Search Engine Marketing):** A broader term than SEO, encompassing both paid search (PPC) and SEO.

**SMM (Social Media Marketing):** The use of social media platforms and websites to promote a product or service.

**SMART Goals:** Specific, Measurable, Achievable, Relevant, Time-bound goals.

**SOP (Standard Operating Procedure):** A set of step-by-step instructions compiled by an organization to help workers carry out routine operations.

**SPOC (Single Point of Contact):** An individual designated as the primary liaison for communication regarding a specific project or issue.

**Standee:** A self-standing display board, often branded, used for advertising or information at events or retail locations. (POS material, BTL).

**Street Team:** A group of promoters or brand ambassadors deployed in public areas (e.g., streets, parks) to engage directly with consumers. (BTL)

**SWOT Analysis:** A strategic planning technique used to identify Strengths, Weaknesses, Opportunities, and Threats related to business competition or project planning.

# T

**Target Audience (TG):** The specific group of consumers or businesses that a company aims to reach with its marketing efforts.

**TAT (Turnaround Time):** The amount of time taken to complete a process or fulfill a request.

**Top-Line Growth:** An increase in a company's gross sales or revenues.

**Trade Marketing:** Marketing activities focused on increasing demand at the wholesale, retail, or distributor level, rather than directly with the end consumer.

**Trial:** The act of a consumer trying a product or service, often encouraged through sampling or free offers.

**TTL (Through-The-Line):** A marketing strategy that integrates both ATL and BTL approaches to create a holistic campaign, often leveraging digital channels to bridge the gap.

# U

**Unique Selling Proposition (USP):** The unique benefit a company, service, product, or brand offers to customers.

**User Experience (UX):** The overall experience of a person using a product, such as a website or computer application, especially in terms of how easy or pleasing it is to use.

**UTM (Urchin Tracking Module) Parameters:** Tags added to URLs to track the source, medium, and campaign of website traffic, useful for measuring digital integration in BTL.

# V

**Value Proposition:** A promise of value to be delivered, communicated, and acknowledged. It is also a belief from the customer about how value will be delivered, experienced, and acquired.

**Vendor Management:** The process of overseeing and managing relationships with suppliers and service providers to ensure they meet contractual obligations and deliver value.

**Visibility Audit:** An assessment of the prominence and effectiveness of branding and merchandising materials in a given retail or market environment.

# Point of Sale Materials (POSM) and Their Use

Point of Sale Materials (POSM) are promotional tools and displays used in retail environments to attract customer attention, highlight products, communicate offers, and ultimately influence purchasing decisions at the exact moment of sale. They are a critical component of BTL and in-store marketing.

POSM are crucial because they act as silent salespeople, reinforcing marketing messages at the most critical point of the customer journey – the moment of purchase. Effective POSM are visually appealing, strategically placed, and clearly communicate a compelling message.

Here are common types of POSM and their uses:

## Danglers / Wobblers:

**Description:** Small, lightweight signs that hang from shelves or ceilings, often designed to sway or "wobble" with air currents, catching the eye.

**Use:** To highlight special offers, new product launches, or specific product features directly above or near the product on the shelf. Their movement makes them highly noticeable.

## Shelf Strips / Shelf Talkers:

**Description:** Narrow, horizontal strips of material that attach to the edge of a retail shelf, directly in front of the product.

**Use:** To display prices, promotions, product benefits, or brand slogans right at the point of decision, guiding the customer's eye to a specific item.

## Standees / Cut-outs:

**Description:** Free-standing, often life-sized (or larger) cardboard or rigid material displays, typically featuring a product, brand mascot, or promotional message.

**Use:** To create a strong visual presence, attract attention from a distance, or serve as a photo opportunity, often placed at store entrances, aisles, or near product displays.

## Posters / Wall Graphics/Painting:

**Description:** Printed signs or graphics affixed to walls, windows, or pillars within the store.

**Use:** To announce promotions, showcase lifestyle imagery, reinforce brand messaging, or direct customers to specific sections.

## FSDUs (Free Standing Display Units) / Gondola Ends:

**Description:** Self-contained, branded display units that stand independently on the store floor, often at the end of aisles (gondola ends) or in high-traffic areas.

**Use:** To create dedicated product zones, promote impulse buys, launch new products with high visibility, or offer bundled deals. They allow for creative product presentation.

## Leaflet Holders / Brochure Stands:

**Description:** Displays designed to hold and dispense informational leaflets, brochures, or coupons.

**Use:** To provide customers with detailed information about a product, service, or ongoing promotion that they can take with them.

## Countertop Displays:

**Description:** Smaller display units designed to sit on checkout counters, service desks, or small display tables.

**Use:** To promote impulse purchases of small items, highlight loyalty programs, or offer last-minute deals right where the transaction occurs.

## Floor Graphics / Decals:

**Description:** Adhesive graphics applied directly to the store floor.

**Use:** To guide customer traffic, highlight promotions, or create an immersive brand experience within an aisle or specific area.

**Wobblers:** (Often used interchangeably with Danglers, but can specifically refer to a sign attached to a flexible plastic strip that "wobbles".)

**Description:** A small sign attached to a spring or flexible plastic strip, allowing it to "wobble" or "spring" out from a shelf.

**Use:** Similar to danglers, they are designed for maximum eye-catching movement to draw attention to specific products or offers on a shelf.

## Shelf Dividers:

**Description:** Branded panels used to separate different products or brands on a shelf.

**Use:** To clearly delineate product categories, highlight a specific brand's section, and improve shelf organization and visual appeal.

## Window Clings / Decals:

**Description:** Adhesive graphics applied to store windows, visible from outside.

**Use:** To announce promotions, new arrivals, store hours, or general brand messaging to passersby, enticing them to enter the store.

## Digital Screens / LED Displays:

**Description:** Electronic screens playing promotional videos, rotating ads, or interactive content.

**Use:** To provide dynamic, engaging, and updatable content, often used for high-impact promotions, product demonstrations, or brand storytelling in modern retail environments.

# EMPOWERING ON-GROUND IMPACT WITH AI

Your Guide to Smarter, Localized, and High-Conversion Campaigns

## SECTION 1: ROLE OF AI IN MODERN BTL CAMPAIGNS

**Key Areas where AI Simplifies BTL Marketing:**

### Audience Segmentation & Personalization:

**Hyper-segmentation:** AI can analyze vast datasets (demographics, purchase history, online behavior, loyalty program data) to create highly granular customer segments beyond traditional categories.

**Personalized Content & Offers:** AI generates tailored messages, offers, and product recommendations for individual customers, making BTL communications feel more relevant and impactful.

**Predictive Analytics:** Predicts future customer behavior, such as churn risk, likelihood to purchase specific products, or preferred communication channels, enabling proactive BTL strategies.

### Content Creation & Optimization:

**Generative AI for Copy:** Creates compelling headlines, ad copy for direct mailers, email subject lines, and scripts for in-store promotions, saving time and ensuring consistency.

**Visual Content Generation:** AI tools can design graphics for flyers, posters, social media ads supporting BTL campaigns, and even short videos for experiential displays.

**Dynamic Content Optimization:** A/B testing and AI-driven optimization of creative elements (e.g., imagery, call-to-actions) in real-time for direct response campaigns.

### Experiential & Event Marketing:

**Personalized Event Experiences:** AI can guide interactive displays, recommend activities to attendees based on their profiles, or offer personalized pathways through an event.

**Sentiment Analysis (during events):** Analyze social media mentions or direct feedback from attendees in real-time to gauge sentiment and make immediate adjustments to an event.

**Resource Optimization:** Predict staffing needs, optimize booth layouts, and manage inventory for event giveaways based on anticipated footfall and audience preferences.

**Post-Event Engagement:** Automate personalized follow-up emails, surveys, and content delivery based on attendee interactions at the event.

### Direct Marketing (Mail, Email, SMS):

**Automated Campaign Management:** Schedule and execute multi-channel direct marketing campaigns, optimizing send times and frequencies based on AI-predicted engagement.

**Subject Line & Call-to-Action Optimization:** AI can generate and test various subject lines and CTAs to maximize open rates and conversions for emails and SMS.

**Dynamic Email Content:** Personalize email content based on recipient behavior, preferences, and real-time data.

In-Store Promotions & Retail Activation:

**Promotion Optimization:** AI can analyze sales data, seasonality, and customer behavior to recommend optimal discounts, product placements, and promotional timings.

**Inventory Management:** Predict demand for promotional items, helping avoid stockouts or overstocking.

**Visual Merchandising Analysis:** AI-powered computer vision can analyze in-store displays, identify compliance issues, and suggest improvements for better product visibility and customer flow.

**Personalized In-Store Experiences:** Using beacons or in-store Wi-Fi, AI can push personalized offers or information to customers' phones as they browse.


# SECTION 2: AI TOOLKIT FOR BTL CAMPAIGNS
## AI Apps & Tools to Simplify BTL Work:

Here are some categories of AI tools and specific examples that can be beneficial for BTL marketing. Keep in mind that many platforms are integrating AI capabilities, so look for "AI-powered" features in your existing marketing tech stack.

A. General AI Marketing & Automation Platforms (often with strong BTL applications):

**HubSpot (with AI-powered Content Assistant, Sales Hub's conversational intelligence):** Excellent for CRM, email marketing, marketing automation, and now with AI for content generation and sales insights. Strong for managing direct customer relationships.

**ActiveCampaign:** Powerful marketing automation platform with AI for predictive sending, lead scoring, and personalized customer journeys, highly effective for email and SMS BTL.

**Optimove:** Uses AI to understand customer behavior, segment audiences, and recommend optimal communication strategies across various channels, including direct marketing.

**Mailchimp (with AI features):** While known for email, it's expanding into broader marketing automation with AI to personalize campaigns and optimize send times.

**Zapier / Make (formerly Integromat):** No-code automation platforms that can connect various AI tools and automate workflows. For example, integrate a lead capture tool at an event with an AI-powered email sequencer.

### B. AI for Content Creation (for BTL collateral):

**Jasper AI / Copy.ai / Writesonic:** Generative AI tools for writing compelling copy for direct mail pieces, email newsletters, SMS campaigns, event descriptions, and promotional slogans.

**Canva (with Magic Studio/AI features):** User-friendly design tool with AI capabilities to quickly create visuals for flyers, posters, social media content, and digital displays.

**Midjourney / DALL-E 3 / Stable Diffusion:** AI image generators for creating unique and eye-catching visuals for your BTL campaigns, especially for experiential marketing where novelty is key.

**Synthesia / Lumen5:** AI video generation platforms to create short, engaging videos for in-store displays, event promotions, or even personalized video messages in direct marketing.

### C. AI for Data Analysis & Personalization:

**Google Analytics (with AI insights):** Provides insights into website and app user behavior, which can inform BTL strategies. Google's ad solutions also leverage AI for targeted advertising (which can drive traffic to BTL touchpoints).

**Brand24 / Mention:** Social listening tools with AI-powered sentiment analysis. Useful for understanding public perception of your BTL events or promotions in real-time.

**GWI Spark:** AI-powered market research tool for deep consumer insights, helping to refine your audience targeting for BTL efforts.

**Adobe Experience Platform (AEP):** An AI-driven data management and customer experience platform that unifies B2C and B2B data for personalized interactions, crucial for complex BTL activations.

**Retalon / Peak (for Retail Promotion Optimization):** AI-powered software specifically designed for retail promotions, optimizing discounts, product placement, and inventory for in-store BTL.

### D. AI for Customer Interaction (relevant for events & in-store):

**Chatfuel / Drift / HubSpot Chatbot Builder:** AI-powered chatbots for engaging with customers at events (via QR codes, apps) or on landing pages promoting BTL activities, answering FAQs, and capturing leads.

**Userbot.ai:** Focuses on conversation management, which can be useful for handling inquiries related to BTL campaigns.

## SECTION 3: AI-ENHANCED BTL CAMPAIGN WORKFLOW

1. Identify Audience: Predictive analytics via CRM
2. Location Selection: Use Placer.ai data
3. Creative Collateral: Generate via Canva AI + ChatGPT
4. On-ground Execution: Use trained reps with tablets or QR codes
5. Lead Capture: Input into Zoho CRM
6. Follow-Up: Voicebot or WhatsApp bot (Skit.ai / Yellow.ai)
7. Measurement: Dashboards and sentiment tools (MonkeyLearn)

## SECTION 4: IMPLEMENTING AI IN BTL MARKETING - BEST PRACTICES:

**Start Small:** Begin with a specific BTL challenge you want to address with AI (e.g., personalizing direct mail, optimizing in-store promotions).

**Define Clear Goals:** What do you want to achieve? (e.g., increase event attendance by X%, boost conversion rate on direct mail by Y%).

**Integrate Data:** The more data you feed into AI tools, the smarter they become. Ensure your customer data is clean and accessible.

**Human Oversight is Key:** AI is a powerful assistant, but human creativity, strategy, and ethical considerations remain paramount, especially in personalized and experiential BTL.

**Test and Learn:** Continuously monitor the performance of your AI-powered BTL campaigns and iterate based on the results.

**Privacy and Ethics:** Be mindful of data privacy regulations (e.g., GDPR, CCPA) when collecting and using customer data for personalization. Transparency with customers is essential.

By strategically integrating AI into your BTL marketing efforts, you can achieve greater personalization, efficiency, and measurable impact, ultimately leading to stronger customer connections and better ROI.

AI is not replacing BTL—it is reinventing it. The smarter your tools, the deeper your human connection.

www.ingramcontent.com/pod-product-compliance
Lightning Source LLC
Chambersburg PA
CBHW052013240626
47153CB00008B/2853